Envy of Angels

D1114492

Also by Matt Wallace

The Failed Cities

Slingers

The Next Fix (collection)

ENVY OF ANGELS

MATT WALLACE

A TOM DOHERTY ASSOCIATES BOOK

NEW YORK

This is a work of fiction. All of the characters, organizations, and events portrayed in this novella are either products of the author's imagination or are used fictitiously.

ENVY OF ANGELS

Copyright © 2015 by Matt Wallace

Cover photo by Getty Images
Cover design by Peter Lutjen

Edited by Lee Harris

All rights reserved.

A Tor.com Book
Published by Tom Doherty Associates, LLC
175 Fifth Avenue
New York, NY 10010

www.tor.com

Tor® is a registered trademark of Tom Doherty Associates, LLC.

ISBN 978-1-4668-9282-8 (e-book)
ISBN 978-0-7653-8528-4 (trade paperback)

First Edition: October 2015

For Nikki, my real-life sin du jour

PART I

DELIVERY DAY

SHOPPING TRIP

A hotel room in São Paulo is the third worst place in the world in which to go into cardiac arrest.

The absolute worst place in the world in which to go into cardiac arrest, based solely on distance and the law of averages, is the middle of the Sahara desert.

The second-worst place is any hospital listed on your HMO plan.

Sao Paulo, however, remains a close third, and has for the better part of a half century.

When Ritter walks out of the small bathroom, towel around his waist, Moon is sprawled motionless over the foot of the bed, his eyes wide and catatonic.

Cindy is bent over him, calmly performing chest compressions.

"What the hell?"

"He ate the whole goddamn tray," Cindy informs him.

Ritter looks over at the tray that had been filled with silver spiny insect eggs when he entered the bathroom.

The same tray is now a pile of cracked, empty pods.

He looks back at Cindy. "He was just supposed to try one!"

"I turned my back for, like, three seconds!" she snaps at him.

Ritter rushes over to two large suitcases resting on the floor against the wall. He crouches down and flips open both.

Inside one is a meticulous arrangement of medical supplies, bandages, syringes, and various scrip bottles. Inside the other is an even more meticulously arranged collection of occult objects ranging from skulls to crystal balls to talismans of a dozen religious and tribal origins.

"Is it a physical reaction or a mystical effect?" he asks over his shoulder.

"His heart's failing!"

Ritter nods. He roots through their traveling emergency room and comes up with a shot of adrenaline sealed in plastic and a portable defibrillator.

Returning to the bed, he removes two adhesive strips tethered to the device's control box by wires. Peeling off their yellow lining, Ritter attaches them both to Moon's slight chest.

He watches the power bar, a series of red tabs slowly converting to blue as the defibrillator charges.

It's four red tabs away from full charge when someone begins steadily and forcefully knocking on their hotel room door.

"What the fuck now!" Cindy explodes.

Ritter silently hands her the control box and steps off the bed.

He's less than three feet from the door when it busts its hinges and comes toppling down onto him, flattening Ritter to the cheaply carpeted floor.

He peers over the top of the door to find bulbous, angry eyes staring back at him.

A six-foot praying mantis is perched on the battered-down wooden slab.

And it is pissed.

Cindy drops over the side of the bed, ready to pounce on the gargantuan insect.

"Stay there!" Ritter orders her, and she halts in her tracks instantly. "Don't let Moon fall out!"

The mantis swings its head up to regard Cindy.

He can feel its weight shifting on the other side of the door, bladed limbs preparing to launch it at her.

Ritter presses the flat of his fist against his side of the door, his mind creating a light-speed montage of memories from a summer he spent as a young martial arts student in his basement mastering Bruce Lee's infamous one-inch punch.

His father called it a stupid waste of time.

Neither of them, of course, could have ever predicted

the career path that has led Ritter to this particular moment and situation.

His fist punches through the cheap wood and grabs a handful of the creature's thorax.

Its shriek is a chorus of nails being swallowed by a garbage disposal.

Cindy hesitates for one brief moment, then leaps up onto the bed, jumping over Moon and grabbing the defibrillator's control box.

It's one tab away from full charge.

"How the fuck did this thing track us here?" Ritter yells out as he struggles to maintain his grip on the mantis.

Cindy's eyes remain glued to the power bar. "Maternal instinct?"

"These things produce hundreds of clutches a fucking year!"

"Yeah, who knew?"

The mantis swipes at Ritter's head, but he manages to duck back beneath the door just before the insect shreds a two-foot expanse of carpet.

"I don't hear Moon not being dead!" he shouts at her.

"In a second!"

Cindy waits.

The last tab on the power bar turns blue.

The defibrillator is fully charged.

She jams her thumb against its large orange button.

Moon's pasty, frail body jumps.

He exhales.

He coughs.

His eyes open.

"That was some good shit," he croaks.

Meanwhile, the splintered door ceases to thunder and crash atop Ritter's body.

He realizes that's because the mantis has stopped thrashing atop the door.

The insect's severed, angular head bounces off the carpet a foot from where Ritter is sprawled out.

Hara pulls the door off Ritter with one hand covered in brown syrupy sludge, holding the slab up against its battered frame.

Ritter lifts his head to regard the stoic giant.

"Did you get the salgadinhos?" he asks.

Hara nods, holding up the paper bag filled with the fried doughy snacks in his other hand.

"Oh, sweet," Ritter says, and his head drops back onto the torn-up carpet.

He closes his eyes.

A few feet away he feels more than he hears Cindy's booted feet touching down on the floor.

Ritter opens his eyes to look at her, upside down, sitting on the side of the bed.

She looks pensive.

"What?" he asks expectantly.

She shakes her head.

"What?" he demands.

"I don't want to be the one to say it."

"You never do."

"We have to go find more eggs now."

Ritter sighs, forcing his body to sit up.

At least three of his ribs are cracked.

"How bad does Bronko really need these things, you figure?"

"Bad enough to expense this whole trip without bitching."

He looks over at the head of the mantis.

Ritter reaches out and flicks one of its bulbous eyes.

"I hope you have a sister," he says.

THE CALL

Lena watches Darren pour rum into the batter for what should be half a second at most and turns into a full five, which in booze-pouring terms might as well be an eternity, particularly in the case of 101-proof Jamaican kick-ass.

"If you want to get schwasted we can just drink, you know."

"This is the therapeutic part," Darren explains as he begins rapidly stirring the batter into dough.

Lena reaches over and snatches the rum bottle from the spot on the counter where he set it aside.

"Right," she says, taking a drink and immediately making that I've-just-poisoned-my-face face.

He's standing in the kitchen of the apartment they share while she sits at the bar separating it from their living area. It's a modest place ("crack-hole was the word she'd used to describe it when they walked through it for the first time), b"ut they've fixed it up to the best of their abilities and they keep it clean. It's theirs, and they've always been proud of it.

They'd known each other in high school, although they weren't close. But there was a mutual respect and recognition that neither of them really fit in.

After high school and three years of "studying abroad," as Lena refers to it, she decided to go to New York and try to break in as a chef. Darren had spent those intervening years in culinary school and was ready to head east himself. Lena contacted him after reading his post about it on Facebook, and the two quickly found they had all the important things in common.

They never really talked about sharing an apartment. Darren simply told her he'd keep an eye out for her as he vetted places for himself. Three months later they were carting the few boxes of their meager belongings up the three flights of stairs to a two-bedroom unit in Williamsburg. Theirs is a vaguely bohemian Brooklyn neighborhood populated by a large number of very chill Ecuadorians.

Darren begins forming pieces of dough into long, thin twists and arranging them on a baking sheet he's greased with butter.

Lena continues to watch him dubiously, taking more careful sips from the bottle.

One of the characters in Darren's favorite series of novels about chefs makes cheese straws when they're nervous.

Darren has borrowed the habit.

"You're going to have to call them eventually," Lena reminds him.

"I know," Darren says quietly as he slides the baking sheet into the preheated oven and slams the door closed.

"Them" are Darren's parents.

It's a concern with which Lena has no ability to empathize. She has a mother in St. Louis she checks in with a few times a year—more like acquaintances than family. She hasn't spoken to her father, who does not live in St. Louis, since she turned eighteen.

Darren's parents, on the other hand, call him twice a week like clockwork, the both of them on speakerphone. They're relentlessly upbeat and supportive, but sometimes more invested in Darren's daily life than even he is. Sometimes to Lena the calls sound more like he's being interviewed than talking to his family.

"We can keep looking," she offers.

"For what? You want to go back to working the line at Bubba-Gump Shrimp Company? No high-end restaurant in the city is going to put us on. That's what 'blackballed' means, El."

"We could try Jersey."

Darren stops forming the next batch of cheese straws and shoots her a look that asks why she'd insinuate such a nasty and disparaging thing about his lineage.

Lena snorts laughter into the mouth of the bottle before taking her next tentative swig.

Darren's iPhone begins playing Eddie Murphy's immortal pop classic "Party All the Time."

Darren often says the ring tone is the gayest thing about him.

Lena always corrects him by saying it's the second-gayest thing.

Darren picks the phone up off the counter and reads the number.

"Shit," he says. "It's a city area code."

Lena's eyebrows inch up.

No one they know with a New York City area code is still speaking to them.

He puts the call on speaker for them both to hear and answers cordially, "Darren Vargas."

"What's up, Darren? This is Byron Luck. I'm the executive chef of Sin du Jour."

Darren quickly mouths the latter name at Lena, who can only shake her head.

"I'm sorry, I'm not familiar with your restaurant. Is it in Manhattan?"

"We're actually a private catering and event company based in Long Island City. At least until the developers come for us with a big-ass check and a wrecking ball. It's amazing where folks want to live these days."

Darren and Lena both laugh, genuinely.

Whoever the chef is, he has a confident, easy way about him.

Although he also sounds busy and preoccupied in the way executive chefs always are.

"Is . . ."—a pause—" . . . Lena Tarr there? You guys room together, right?"

They trade more confused looks above the phone.

"Um. Yeah. Yes. She's right here, actually. You're on speaker."

"Hey, Lena."

"Hey."

"So are you two a couple?"

"No," Darren says quickly. "We're just roommates. We've been friends since high school."

"Cute. Look, I find myself suddenly short-staffed with a massive event coming up. We're actually already prepping for it. I could use both of you on the line tomorrow, if you're available. I'll need you for at least a week, maybe more."

Neither of them can believe the offer he's just made, and it shows on their faces.

"Wow. That's . . . crazy."

"If you don't mind my asking, not that I'm not . . . or we're not interested—we are—but how did you get our names and my number?"

"Tunney told me about you guys," Luck explains easily, completely unruffled. "He said you're top hands. He said you got a raw deal over at that shiny splooge factory you were fired from. Porto Fiero or Fucko or whatever."

They both grin at his description of their former place of employment, and at the mention of Tunney, the ancient dishwasher with whom they shared their only good times there.

"You worked with Tunney?" Darren asks.

"He worked for me. Once upon a fuckin' time."

"Excuse me," Lena chimes in. "Are you . . . Bronko Luck?"

"It's mostly just Byron now," he answers without hesitation, "but yeah, I was. Again, once upon a fuckin' time."

Lena appears genuinely stunned.

"I'm sorry, but I thought . . ."

"You thought I died."

"Yeah. Sorry."

"Don't worry about it. I did. Briefly. So, are you up for it? The both of you? Tunney told me what you were making. I'll put a cherry on top of that, say twenty percent."

Darren and Lena regard each other, but there's really no discussion to be had, silent or otherwise.

"Yeah, absolutely."

Darren seconds that. "Yes, sir."

"Good. I'll text you the address. I need you here at six.

If you're late you're not on my line."

Together: "Yes, Chef."

"That's what I like to hear. See you both at sunrise."

He ends the call.

They're silent for a moment, both processing the abruptness of what's just happened.

Then Darren says, "Who the fuck is Bronko Luck?"

"You don't remember? He had all those gastropubs when we were in school, Dead Man's Hand. And his restaurant here was called the Monkey's Paw. He was, like, famous. Sorta Bobby Flay meets Guy Fieri, only—"

"Less douchey?"

"Yeah."

"I wasn't keeping track of shit like that back then, I guess. What did he say about dying? Or what did you say?"

"That's what I remember reading. He was presumed dead. His restaurant closed. The pub chain got sold off and turned into Applebee's or whatever the hell."

"Jesus."

"Yeah."

"I mean . . . it's a catering company."

"In Long Island City," Lena adds.

"In Long Island City. Still, catering—"

"Dude, we got a new job."

"We did. You're right."

Lena suddenly climbs over the table and seizes Darren around the shoulders.

"I don't have to call them!" he practically screeches, spinning her.

When they're done reveling, Darren looks around at the baking fallout all over the counters, and at the hot oven.

"What am I going to do with all this shit now?" he asks.

Lena shrugs. "Landlord?"

Darren shrugs back. "Fuck it. We're employed again."

"Yeah. Hey, what did he say the place is called?"

SIN DU JOUR

The place they're looking for is a three-story rectangle of dusty red brick piled on the corner of an obscure industrial block far from the nearest residential building development (they're becoming a plague, it seems). Circling it in Darren's beat-to-shit Dodge Neon, they missed the building twice before finally spotting the small faded sign bolted above the front entrance.

It's not exactly what they expected from a former celebrity chef. The logo features a decadent piece of chocolate cake with cartoon limbs and a smiling cartoon face. SIN DU JOUR CATERING & EVENTS is stenciled around it in a trying-too-hard-to-be-elegant font whose letters are peeling from age.

They regard each other, Darren with trepidation and Lena with pure skepticism, which is usually how their reactions split from each other's.

They're here, however, and they need whatever work is waiting inside this strange edifice. They've both come dressed for battle, toting their knife cases. Lena is already donning the headband she always wears in the kitchen, with its sweat-faded logo against her pixie-cut scalp. Darren opts, when allowed, to tuck his own messy black locks under his lucky Taft High Falcons baseball cap spun backward.

"Maybe it's some kind of new reality show," Darren offers as they approach the front doors. "You know, find young, hot, down-on-their-shitty-luck chefs and bring them to some weird-ass building in the middle of nowhere and surprise them."

"I notice you tossed 'hot' in there."

"I was talking about me."

"Of course."

"Of course."

They both laugh, and it helps ease the tension and allay their fears long enough to walk inside the building.

The lobby of Sin du Jour is the exact opposite of its façade: it's modern, expensively decorated, and meticulously kept. Lena's immediate thought, albeit absently, is that the outside almost seems like camouflage—an odd choice for a business serving such a competitive industry.

They're met with a circular reception desk lacking a receptionist. A broad picture window behind it looks out onto a stone courtyard that must exist in the center of the whole structure.

Lena and Darren idle in the lobby, unsure of what to do next.

It's not as if they can ring a bell for service.

They mill about for a while, each anticipatory moment agonizingly drawn out. Darren conspiratorially peers down the long hallway leading off from the lobby, but chickens out short of actually stepping down it.

He feels Lena judging him with her eyes, so he doesn't look at her.

Thankfully they begin to hear voices growing louder and moving in their direction. They soon realize it is a single voice accompanied by the loud, steady clacking of heels-on-floor.

A tall, lithe woman appears from the deep hallway beyond the empty reception desk. She's wearing a very smart Chanel knock-off suit and what must be three hundred dollars' worth of high-end makeup and grooming products. On her left ear is affixed what must be the tiniest Bluetooth ever conceived by man. She looks more West Coast than East to both Lena and Darren, right down to a perfect tan.

That's when they notice the small fleshy growth that covers most of her left ear.

Darren and Lena both find the floor suddenly fascinating and proceed to study it thusly.

"—I'm not producing a high school prom on Staten Island, Rico," the woman says, continuing her conversation from the hallway. "This is an extremely important diplomatic function, and the onus to remember that is yours. Now get it done."

She taps her Bluetooth without waiting for a reply, and although she was standing in front of them both for the last ten seconds of the call she only now acknowledges their presence.

"You must be the replacement cooks," she says with a businesslike smile.

Darren and Lena have used the time to discern how to look at her directly without focusing on her other ear.

Well, mostly figure it out, anyway.

"Yeah. Yes. I'm Darren. This is Lena."

"It's a pleasure to meet you both. My name is Jett Hollinshead. I'm the event coordinator here. Welcome to Sin du Jour."

They all shake hands.

"Byron was right behind me." Jett glances behind herself, confused, before looking back at them. "We really appreciate you coming on short notice."

"We appreciate the opportunity, trust me," Darren says.

Lena nods, but her thoughts have another focus. "You were saying this is a 'diplomatic' event we're cooking for?"

"Ah, yes. I really should let Byron fill you in on any details—"

"I got it, Jett," the same voice that spoke to them over the phone last night says from the reception area.

Chef Byron "Bronko" Luck has a nose that's been broken more than once and white threads engaged in an active siege against his otherwise dark hair. He's also much wider than Lena recalls from the pictures in his heyday, although whether he's gained weight or her memory subtracted it she isn't sure.

"You're on time," he says in lieu of a greeting. "That's good."

Darren nods eagerly. "Of course, Chef."

"We're in the weeds, so let's get you going, okay?"

"We're ready, Chef," Lena says. "But Miss Hollinshead here was just telling us about the event. It's a diplomatic—"

Her next word recoils with the rest of her body as the window behind the reception desk abruptly shatters and a small, wiry body flies through its wake, bouncing off the top of the reception desk and rolling across the carpet between all of them.

"Holy shit!" Darren cries out.

What turns out to be a twentysomething man dressed like a bike messenger rights himself on the carpet in front of them.

"Whoa," he says through ragged breaths.

Chef Luck strides around the reception desk. "Goddammit, Pac!" he yells out the window. "How many times with this shit?"

From the courtyard, a young, slightly dazed voice answers him: "If I don't put them through their paces I'm not doing my due diligence, boss!"

"I'll put your smoked-out skull through paces, you little prick!"

"Sorry, boss!"

Grumbling and suddenly tense through his chest, Chef Luck returns to the stunned Darren and Lena and Jett, who looks more embarrassed than anything.

"You okay?" Chef asks the kid sitting on the floor.

"My bad," the kid says.

He stands, shakily for a moment, but finds his feet. There are several small but noticeable cuts on his forearms, but he seems otherwise uninjured.

Without another word he's on his feet and bounds back over the reception desk. He leaps and forms himself into a tight ball, gliding back out through the window effortlessly.

Darren and Lena watch him go.

They look to Chef Luck with hanging jaws.

"Our servers," he explains. "They have . . . their own audition process."

Darren just nods dumbly.

Lena has that skeptical look she often gets.

"Our events are demanding on the support staff," Jett adds brightly. "I'll see to this, Byron."

"Yeah. Thanks, Jett."

The chef is ready to address them further when the front doors open (normally and without violent force) behind Darren and Lena.

They turn to watch a quartet of people shuffling tiredly inside. Darren briefly marks them as homeless before dismissing that idea, albeit just barely. They look bedraggled to the point of ruin. Their clothes have all been torn in various places, their faces and hands are smudged with some kind of dirt or muck, and several of them wear bandages over seeping wounds.

A small, mousey-looking man with his shirt ripped open is leaning heavily on one of the largest human beings either Darren or Lena has ever seen. The giant is holding the control box of what looks like a mobile defibrillator, while its pads are stuck to the mousey one's almost nonexistent chest.

Standing in front of them are a muscular woman with her tawny hair fashioned into cornrows and a hard-looking man with the end of a lit cigarette dangling from his lips, who might be terribly attractive if he weren't currently so unkempt.

He's hoisting a military surplus-looking ruck bulging in several dozen places over his shoulder.

"What the hell happened to Moon?" Chef Luck asks the tall, rangy man standing in front of the group.

The man just shakes his head, the half-burnt cigarette bobbing side-to-side precariously.

"Okay, then," Chef says. "As long as he's good."

"Hara's got him."

The colossal man behind them holds up the defibrillator control reassuringly.

"I like what you've done with your hair, Cindy," Jett says to the woman. "Is that new?"

"Only every time we go out, Jett," she says.

"Oh."

The unshaven man looks at Darren and Lena, then at Chef Luck.

"Newbies?" he asks.

Chef nods.

The man nods in return.

He motions to his fellows, and they all collectively file out around Darren and Lena without another word or a glance.

"That was Ritter, our steward," Jett explains a little too quickly. "He's head of stocking and receiving. I believe they were picking up some supplies downtown. Special ingredients for our current event's menu. You know."

"Right," Chef says. "It's a dangerous part of town, that farmers' market."

He jerks his head at Darren and Lena.

"You two, with me."

Chef Luck doesn't wait for them. He turns and begins striding back up the hallway from which he first appeared.

They're left with no time to process any one of the several freakish events they've just witnessed, let alone all of them together.

They exchange a brief look whose implication is that their rent isn't any less due because of those events.

They rush to catch up.

As they walk through the halls of Sin du Jour, a small brindle-and-white Shih Tzu chewing on a chicken bone scurries around Chef Luck's legs and bounds between Darren and Lena.

"Is that your puppy, Chef?" Darren asks, a little more excitedly than he probably would've liked.

"No, it's a damn stray one of my people took to feeding this morning."

"Is that sanitary?" Lena asks.

"Not even a little, no. I've told my crew to keep him out of the kitchen. You two do the same."

Darren shoots her a look. "I thought you liked dogs."

"I like hounds. Shih Tzus are like Ewoks with underbites."

They're not sure, but ahead of them it sounds like

Chef chortles.

They pass a tall, wide arch through which is what looks to be the main Sin du Jour kitchen. There are at least half a dozen cooks busily attending the gleaming, state-of-the-art equipment. Darren and Lena's natural instinct is to stop and linger, but Chef Luck never breaks stride, never even slows down. They snatch a moment's pause and several brief glances before rushing to catch up.

For the briefest moment Lena makes eye contact with who is noticeably the tallest cook in the kitchen. She only has time to notice one thing: that his five o'clock shadow is hours too early and also too light to be left over from the day before, which means it's a look he cultivates.

It strikes her he has the exact opposite air of Ritter, who looked to have earned every bit of his disheveled appearance.

She immediately files the cook's image under "asshole" in her mind and moves on.

Chef Luck leads them into what looks to be a small test kitchen away from the main action of the catering prep.

They immediately take note of two large pineapples resting in the center of side-by-side cutting boards on the nearest workstation.

"It's audition time, kids," the chef announces.

"I thought we had the gig," Lena says.

"I said I needed you and for how long. And I do need you. But only if you can hack it. This isn't Porto Fancy-fuck. This here is being in the weeds from dawn till dusk, every day, all day."

"We drove all the way over here from Brooklyn, Chef," Darren says, more pleading than insisting.

"If you blow the audition, I'll cover your gas and pay you out for the day in full. Fair enough?"

Darren looks to Lena.

They both nod.

What other choice do they have?

Chef Luck places his fingertips atop the counter between the cutting boards.

He looks down at the pineapples.

"I need you to process and then brunoise these fuckers. And I want to see symmetrical cubes too. All the way through."

"Okay," Lena says immediately and with a resolve directed at her rather than him.

"In sixty seconds or less," Chef adds heavily.

That detail of the "audition" might as well be a gauntleted fist socking them directly in their guts.

"That's impossible," Darren says with no attempt to mask his feelings.

"Yeah," Chef Luck says blandly. "It is."

"But—" Darren begins.

"You need three things to work here: ungodly speed and even more precision. This is the best test of both. Not to mention most of what you'll be doing is prep work. We slam it out here, in volume, but we slam it out perfectly every time. That's the standard. If you can't meet it, I can't use you."

"Those are actually only two things," Lena points out, more pissed off than fearful of losing this opportunity. "You only listed two things."

"Yeah, well, you don't need to worry about the third thing. You're just filling in for a few days. So, do you want to skin your knives, or do you want gas money and one day's pay?"

Darren might've thought about it if Lena didn't immediately unzip her case and select a large kitchen knife.

With a deep sigh, he does the same.

"Okay, then."

Chef Luck steps away from the cutting boards.

He removes an antique stopwatch from his pocket.

Lena and Darren step in front of their stations.

The Sin du Jour chefs have begun filtering into the test kitchen, lining the walls, watching and whispering to each other.

They're all grouped around Five O'Clock Shadow, who looks to be their foreman, whether it's self-appointed or otherwise.

Lena notices for the first time that there are no women among them.

"Don't look at them," she instructs Darren under her breath. "Nothing exists but that stupid fucking pineapple in front of you."

"Yes, Mom," he says, but his voice is shaky.

"I don't mean to interrupt your conversation, kids," Chef interjects, "but I just started your time."

"Son of a bitch!" Lena practically growls.

Laughter from the line of cooks standing against the wall.

Darren and Lena attack their pineapples.

Lena's knife skills outmatch Darren's. There's also a military precision and discipline in her every movement.

Darren is technically gifted and precise, even meticulous to a fault, but it makes him noticeably slower than her. He was sweating before the clock even started counting down, and within twenty seconds he looks like the CIA is interrogating him.

They get their pineapples broken down at almost the same times, but when they begin to brunoise Lena takes an immediate and decisive lead. It's not a terribly complicated process: it's basically cutting something into small, uniform cubes.

Doing it both fast and well, however, is a particular

challenge.

Fortunately challenge has defined so much of Lena's life it has become what she lives for, in large part.

At forty-five seconds, Lena slams her knife down on the cutting board and takes one catlike step back.

"Done!" she announces.

One of the chefs standing against the wall, a younger West African man, whistles for her triumphantly.

Her focus immediately shifts to Darren's station.

He's not going to make it.

He's processing one large chunk and still has another set aside he's yet to cube.

Lena doesn't think, doesn't consider, and doesn't hesitate; she steps back up to the station and swipes her knife from her own cutting board. She grabs Darren's final chunk of pineapple and makes six cuts with her knife.

The last tiny cube falls away from each of their chunks just as Chef Luck announces, "Time!"

Lena slams down her knife for a second time, stepping back.

Darren steps back as well, but he's still holding his knife in a trembling hand.

None of the other cooks react.

Chef Luck folds his arms across his mountainous chest and paces around them, examining their work.

After an unnecessarily long time, he turns away from

the stations to face them.

"That wasn't the challenge."

Lena is ready for him. "You said both had to be brunoised in sixty seconds. That's all you said."

Chef looks down at Darren. "You didn't finish, Vargas."

"*We* did," Lena insists.

"I can speak for myself," Darren practically hisses at her.

Chef is waiting on him. "Well?"

Darren thinks for a moment and then says simply, "We finished, Chef."

Chef Luck stares down at Lena. "And if I say you're in and he's out?"

"Then we both go home."

Chef Luck shifts his heavy gaze back to Darren. "And if I say I don't like her attitude, so you can stay?"

"We came to work together, Chef. We're gonna leave together."

Chef Luck nods.

"All right, then. Call me Bronko."

He doesn't shake their hands or clap them on the back, but it's clear they've passed this small initiation, for whatever it's worth.

There's also no applause or further show of approval or support from the other cooks.

"Was that the third thing we need to work here, Bronko?" Lena asks.

"What? Teamwork? Hell, no. Like I said, don't worry about the third thing. Just do as you're told."

"Yes, Chef."

He nods, motioning them over to another station.

There's an array of appetizers spread out on the counter, forks resting beside each.

"This is what you're going to be doing. We need three hundred of each of these. Give 'em a tasting."

Each of the four small dishes in front of them is beautiful to look upon. They both recognize the first three, more or less.

"Dive in," Chef instructs them.

They begin by sampling mini-oxtail taquitos covered with the absolute hottest mole negro either of them has ever tasted.

Chef can't help laughing at their teary-eyed, red-faced reactions.

"Yeah, we call that 'brimstone' mole," he explains.

The second app is a tiny Korean short rib pizza with some type of sriracha-based sauce on top. Its flavor is remarkable, but also overwrought with surprising heat. The third dish is a bite-sized stuffed pepper.

"Who are your clients, Chef?" Lena asks. "Jamaican pepper farmers?"

"They like their heat," he says simply.

The final appetizer is the one that really throws them. It's a small, decorative (they both collectively hope, at least) skull with a bamboo chute protruding from it.

"Use the chute as a straw," Bronko instructs them.

They each take turns at the mouth of the bamboo chute.

Their throats practically disintegrate.

"Holy hell!" Lena yells between bouts of coughing.

"That's a contradiction," Bronko says as he hands them both shot glasses filled with milk.

They both gulp them down gratefully.

"Try it again."

Darren and Lena look at him as though he's insane.

"It's only a pure burn the first time. Try it again. You'll get the flavor."

They do it because a job depends on it, and that's obvious.

But Chef is right; it still burns, but there's a distinct flavor this time.

Its taste fails to find a reference with either of them.

Their eyes agree with each other's that it's delicious.

"What is this?" Darren asks.

"Exotic," is all Bronko says. "Curry, basically. But exotic. Don't worry about what it's called, just so long as you replicate the proportion, plating, and taste exactly."

"Yes, Chef."

Lena looks at Darren, baffled as to how he can accept that.

"But what—"

"That tall drink of water over there," Bronko points at Five O'Clock Shadow, "is Tag Dorsky, my sous-chef. If and when you run out of anything in here, anything at all, you see him. Okay? Neither of you is allowed in my pantry. That's a rule. It is unbreakable. Understood?"

Darren and Lena don't need to share a silent look to agree that's one of the strangest rules they've ever been handed down by an executive chef.

They both nod.

"All right." Bronko turns to his sous-chef and line cooks. "Tag, take 'em through the apps. Then get the hell back to galley. No one sold you assholes tickets to a show here."

"Yes, Chef" is returned in a chorus.

"Good luck, kids," Bronko says to Darren and Lena before walking out of the test kitchen.

Darren and Lena wait.

Dorsky addresses the rest of the line too quietly for them to hear, but it ends with him dispatching them from the test kitchen with another round of laughs.

Lena puts a gold star on his "asshole" file in her mental cabinet.

When the rest of them have gone, Dorsky walks over to them.

"Bronko's getting soft in his golden years. I'd have tossed you both."

"Did you have to do this when you got the job?" Darren asks.

Dorsky grins. "No."

THE FORBIDDEN PANTRY

When Darren tells the story later—and he will, many times—he'll recount how he couldn't be bothered to obey such an absurd directive. He'll paint himself, however subconsciously, as a chef who bucks authority and disobeys orders as a matter of roguish principle.

The truth is that in that moment he's too afraid to talk to the Sin du Jour chefs.

That's all.

After four hours, he and Lena have run out of Chef Luck's mystery ingredient, the "mostly curry" concoction to fill the skulls, and they still have a hundred apps left to prepare.

"I'll go talk to that dick Dorsky," Lena offers. "Dicksky."

She laughs at her own joke.

It's enough to prompt Darren to volunteer himself in her place.

They need this job, both of them.

"Fine," Lena says.

"Just take a break, El. You've slammed out twice as

many of these things as me, anyway."

Lena doesn't comment.

She can't, because it's true.

Darren removes his sweat-soaked hat and leaves the test kitchen, carefully navigating the still unfamiliar halls of Sin du Jour. As he walks down the hall toward the main kitchen, he spots what appears to be the entire line exiting through its archway. They're grouped around Tag Dorsky, laughing and carrying on some conversation that probably began an hour ago.

They must be taking a break, grabbing a smoke or a staff meal.

Darren waits until they've disappeared up the hall and then enters Sin du Jour's main kitchen, cautiously, hoping very much it doesn't look that way to any observer.

Ritter, the man Chef Luck introduced as his steward, and the rest of his put-upon staff are gathered around a refrigeration unit in the corner. They've all helped themselves to what looks to Darren like frozen pistachio mousse push-up pops.

None of them seem to take particular notice of him, and if they do they don't acknowledge him.

Darren strolls (at least he hopes he appears to be strolling) to the back of the kitchen, where the large door to the pantry is located.

He reaches out and grips the door's handle.

He inches it open.

A commotion back near the archway causes him to shut it immediately. His pulse races and his heart pounds, thinking the line cooks have returned from their break.

But it's only two of the servers—a young, skinny, stoner-looking kid and an old man.

They're sneaking that Shih Tzu into the kitchen.

Darren realizes they're stealing food for the stray dog, which appears to have become the staff's unofficial mascot.

They don't seem to notice him either.

It doesn't stop their presence from locking Darren's limbs.

He suddenly realizes how pathetically he's behaving, how frightened and how ridiculous that is. He thinks about how Lena would judge him for it, and how he judges himself even worse.

Darren inhales deeply, pulls open the pantry door, and walks inside.

He feels a brief, wondrous adrenaline rush as he closes the door behind him.

It's followed by abject disappointment.

It's just a pantry.

All he did was walk into a kitchen pantry.

Now he feels even more pathetic.

Darren looks around at the racks of dry spices, the giant sealed tubs of flour and sugar and salt, and the array of produce and dry goods.

He doesn't spot the missing ingredient from his and Lena's cold apps.

Then he notices there's a murky plastic curtain on the other side of the space separating the main pantry from another room.

Darren wanders over, pulls the curtain apart, and steps inside.

This time he is the exact opposite of disappointed.

He's also extremely confused.

This doesn't look like a pantry; it looks like a curio shop.

It reminds Darren of the weird ancient Chinese man's store from the movie *Gremlins,* where the dad finds and buys Gizmo. He thinks about the Monkey's Paw, Chef Luck's famous restaurant in the '90s, and how this is exactly the kind of space in which he might expect to find such an item sitting on a shelf.

Darren moves slowly through the space. He begins to realize that what he's looking at must be exotic ingredients. His hands graze the surface of dozens of large eggs a color and texture he's never before encountered. There's an entire basket of them. He finally spots the unidentified ingredients for their apps. They're resting between a clear plastic container of some type of pickled feet, larger and more terrifying-looking than anything Darren has ever seen, and a bowl of what he doesn't want to believe are eyeballs.

Walking toward the bowl, his eyes are drawn to what looks like a large pickling jar on the middle shelf. The liquid inside is a sickly green, murkier than any pickling juice with which he's familiar.

It's what is being pickled, however, that suddenly captures his full attention.

Darren steps in front of the shelf and tentatively slides a hand behind the jar, inching it forward. What's inside looks whole, and was definitely once a living thing. He wonders if it might be some type of exotic fish, probably Asian. He identifies what he thinks is a sharp-looking fin.

Then he realizes it's not a fin, it's a small bladed limb. And what he thought was a fish looks much more like an insect.

Darren can't fathom what culinary use such a thing might have, and he's wondering now what the hell he and Lena have been cooking with all day, and who might want to eat a dish composed of elements like the ones surrounding him now.

That's when Darren makes the mistake every second-act player in a horror movie makes.

He leans into the glass to examine the specimen more

closely.

Its body turns on a dime within the viscous liquid and a giant black eye seems to blink a million microscopic lids at him rapidly.

Darren jumps back, his hand pulling the jar forward off the shelf.

It tumbles all the way to the floor.

It shatters.

The thing inside, the living thing, begins flopping around on the floor amid glass shrapnel. The motion is very fishlike, despite the now irrefutable fact that this is no type of fish Darren has ever seen on Animal Planet but is very much like an insect from a B movie about atomic radiation run amok. The flopping turns into shaking, and it's almost like a canine trying to shed the water from an unwanted bath; Darren's chef pants are sprinkled with the thick green pickling liquid from the jar.

He's been inching back toward the curtain for the past several seconds, but he suddenly stops, transfixed by a new, horrifying development.

The creature is growing.

Its head is bulging in convulsive spurts, each one leaving it a little larger in diameter. Its skinless body expands in ragged, breathlike motions. Its bladed limbs begin to stretch and stretch. They grow long enough to reach out and impale the lip of the third bottom shelf. The creature begins using the leverage to hoist itself upright.

In seconds it has become the size of a small child.

Darren is no longer aware of his own body.

That's when he hears Lena's voice, calling to him from outside in the kitchen. It tethers him back to the moment and himself, and he manages to slip through the curtain. Once he's beyond sight of the creature he finds the presence and strength to turn and bolt out through the pantry door, closing it behind him.

Lena is waiting for him. At first she looks impatient, even annoyed, but her expression changes immediately when she sees the one he's wearing.

"What's wrong with you?" she asks.

"I didn't . . . I didn't mean . . . Jesus Christ, El, it's—"

His breathing is elevated and he's practically leaping from his own skin.

Across the room, reclining against the refrigerator, Ritter finally takes notice of the young chefs.

He takes particular notice of Darren preparing to hyperventilate.

He walks over to the pantry as Lena grips Darren's shoulders and tries to maneuver him toward a more secluded area of the kitchen.

"Darren, what the hell—"

"You okay, kid?" Ritter asks, approaching them.

"He's fine," Lena insists immediately, defensively.

"Take it easy, all right? This place can be a little freaky on newbies—"

"I said he's fine."

Darren shakes his head, trying to find the words to assure both of them it is definitely *not* fine, but failing to force them past his lips.

Ritter is standing nearest the pantry door when it bursts open and the now-six-foot-tall bladed monster emerges, enraged and seeking revenge for its imprisonment in a small glass jar. Ritter is knocked back against the nearest chef's station.

The shock momentarily paralyzes Darren.

Lena is taken aback, as any rational person accustomed solely to the mortal horrors of the world would be, but her first instinct is to shield Darren.

Ritter's first instinct is to grab the nearest pair of cutting boards and use them to neutralize the creature's razor-edged limbs. He manages to meet the first deadly swipe perfectly, impaling the bone blade deep into the wood of one of the boards. The shriek as the creature struggles in vain to free it is bloodcurdling.

When it swipes with its other primary limb, Ritter moves to engage it the same way.

It's still a good plan.

However, this time he's an eighth of a second too slow.

The next shriek doesn't emanate from the creature.

Lena rushes forward, shouting for help.

Something weighty hits Darren in the chest, breaking him loose of the paralysis.

He immediately and instinctively hugs his arms against his chest, catching and holding the object that just collided with it.

It is soft.

It is warm.

It is hairy.

It is dripping.

Darren looks down.

It is Ritter's severed arm.

THE BOSS

Bronko Luck (despite his insistence that he's "mostly Byron" now, he still thinks of himself as the man who was nicknamed Bronko as a freshman football star) has only mandated two new rules since taking on the mantle of Sin du Jour's executive chef.

The first and most unbreakable is this: Sin du Jour does not, nor will it ever, serve werewolves.

They also don't serve werewolf.

The second rule, which stood unbreakable until today, is this: never disturb Bronko when the door to his office is closed.

He's sitting behind his desk, sorting through purchase orders, some written in languages that don't technically exist, and listening to Leonard Cohen through a pair of high-quality Bose headphones. It's his latest and possibly last album, *Popular Problems,* released on the man's eightieth birthday. Bronko doesn't truck with Mr. Cohen's earlier work; his is the haggard, gravel-voiced Cohen who sounds like he's lived through a million bad decisions that should've killed him.

That has always been Bronko's model for living, and integral to his perception of himself. He's a gambler who bucked popular wisdom at every turn and came out ahead for the risk.

They told him not to put the word "dead" in the name of a restaurant he was trying to brand, that it was guaranteed to kill his idea before the first review.

It became one of the largest and most successful American gastropub chains of the '90s.

They told him calling a high-end restaurant The Monkey's Paw would never fly on the New York scene. They said it was an unappetizing moniker that would remind people of a stew joint in Bangkok.

It won a Michelin star and a James Beard Award, and made Bronko one of the most famous chefs in the country.

They told him not to gamble with a thing as precious and singular as his soul.

He probably should've listened to that one.

In the middle of the bridge to "Samson in New Orleans" the door to his office flies open (it's never locked; fear of Bronko is more impassable than any lock) and Jett rushes in. The clacking of her absurdly high heels is like a battalion furiously striking at a front line of marble-armored enemies.

"Byron!"

Bronko pulls the headphones down around his thick, tattooed neck.

"What in *the* fish oil–soaked hell, Jett?"

"One of the newbies let a diophoid out of the pantry! It's loose in the main kitchen!"

It's as if his face doesn't know which thing to express anger about first, like there's a queue of rage backed up behind Bronko's features congesting any expression.

A cry of "Son of a bastard!" breaks the emotive gridlock and he bounds from his desk chair with a snarl.

As he strides past her, out of his office, and down the hall he can hear Jett clacking frantically after him, but he forgets about her for the moment.

Bronko can hear the eruption in the kitchen from the hall. He pauses just long enough to reach into a janitorial closet and pull out a long broom.

As he nears the entrance he spots the rest of his cooks rushing down the other end of the hall, Dorsky in the lead.

"What the fuck is—"

"Shut up," Bronko cuts off his sous-chef as he rounds the corner of the kitchen's archway.

"Chaos" seems almost a quaint word to describe the state of the kitchen around them. It all escalated very quickly, as chaotic events often do. In one moment Darren was cautiously venturing into the pantry, and in the next moment a creature unlike anything that should exist in the real world (rapidly becoming a questionable concept for Darren) had invaded the kitchen and Ritter was less an arm for his attempt to corral it back into the pantry.

The scene that has evolved from that incident is unlike anything Darren could've imagined before entering the world of Sin du Jour.

An ancient Navajo man and his granddaughter are chanting around an impromptu sand painting they've created out of all-purpose flour spilled on the floor. A full chorus supplements their voices, echoing their chant. It's coming through speakers attached to the girl's iPod. From the snatch of brief, panicked conversation that preceded the event, Darren understands it is supposed to pacify the monster—and that's what it is, a genuine, living, breathing monster from underneath a childhood bed—that just detached Ritter's arm.

The mousey-looking tweaker called Moon has gone into cardiac arrest again and is groping for the control box of the defibrillator pads attached to his chest. The mountainous man who was in charge of the box had to drop it to help corral the monster back into the forbidden pantry. One of the busboys kicks the small, sleek emergency life-saving device over to Moon, who shocks his heart into beating anew for the seventh time that day.

A sound like a gunshot rings out, but it's only Lena, who has just slapped Ritter across the face in an effort to keep him conscious. He's sweating and groaning and squirming against her knee as it braces his bloody stump of a limb against the kitchen floor.

The fingers of Ritter's hand are still twitching sporadically as Darren cradles the severed arm.

The Shih Tzu stray that's been trotting throughout the building all day is barking its head off in the corner. It's an absurdly cute-gruff punctuation to the yells of Cindy and Hara wrestling with the creature from the pantry, Ritter's pained noises, and the Native Americans' chanting.

The servers are standing on either side of the dog, passive and unperturbed. Darren doesn't know how much of that is the joint they're passing back and forth between dueling puffs. They both look like they're watching a bland sitcom, and even occasionally finding it amusing.

Bronko ignores the chaos, the severed arm, the triage being performed on its owner, Moon shocking himself back to life, the barking dog, all of it. He steps over the Native American artwork fashioned in all-purpose flour and through the marijuana din, cutting a direct swath to the pantry door.

Cindy and Hara are grappling with either side of the

diophoid, which is continuing to expand in size. It's almost too big to fit through the pantry door now. Bronko stares into its single bulbous eye, which is actually tens of thousands of microscopic eyes.

It looks pissed, as anything would after being shrunk to the size of a football and stored in a pickling jar.

Bronko grips the broom handle with both hands and spins its long, rectangular head before jamming the bristles into the creature's face.

Its shriek is as inhuman as one would expect a giant insect's shriek to be.

The diophoid recoils from the broom as if the bristles are on fire, allowing Hara and Cindy to stuff it the rest of the way inside the pantry and close the door.

Hara locks it.

He and Cindy look back at Bronko, their breath ragged and their clothing torn.

"Horsehair," he explains softly. "Diophoids are deathly allergic to horsehair."

Hara nods.

Cindy actually grins. There's something rueful and cynical in the way her lips curl.

The kitchen is suddenly mercifully quiet.

Except for the barking of the Shih Tzu.

Bronko shoots an arm in its direction and snaps his meaty fingertips sharply.

The dog stops barking.

Bronko snaps his fingers once more and then points at the floor.

The dog sits.

Bronko nods, satisfied.

"Okay, then," he says.

Dorsky and the other cooks have filled the kitchen archway and are surveying the wreckage of the last fifteen minutes with bewilderment.

Bronko continues ignoring them as he tosses the broom away and kneels beside Ritter, whose face has turned the white of a gravestone in winter.

"How is he?" Bronko asks Lena.

"He's lost a lot of blood, not to mention a fucking arm," she says bitterly. "We need to get him evac'ed to a hospital."

Bronko looks up at Darren, who now appears to be clinging to the severed arm as if it's the only thing anchoring his sanity.

"We'll get his arm reattached, don't worry. He doesn't need a hospital."

"Are you fucking crazy? I had to cauterize it to stop the bleeding; he'll never—"

"Trust me," Bronko assures her.

"Trust you? I should call the cops right—"

"I said," Bronko thunders, "*trust* me."

Something in the command of his voice, something with a firmer grasp of the reality in which they've found themselves than Lena could ever hope to achieve, quells her rage.

"Hang in there, Ritt," Bronko says.

Bronko stands, briefly resting a reassuring hand on Lena's shoulder. He reaches up and pats Darren's cheek, feeling genuine sympathy for the kid, before turning back to Cindy and Hara.

"Go find Boosha and Ryland and get them to put that fucking thing back in its jar before it destroys the whole goddamn pantry, then they can get Ritt's wing back on and working."

"Sure, boss," Cindy says, the two departing the kitchen immediately, double-timing it.

Bronko walks back across the kitchen. White Horse has retrieved the broom the executive chef used to tame the diophoid and is already sweeping up his flour painting. His granddaughter is winding iPod wires around her fingers.

Bronko stops directly in front of Dorsky.

Although the sous-chef is several inches taller, he suddenly looks like a child standing under Bronko's gaze.

"The only reason I don't rip your fuckin' head off and use your skull to serve chowder is I can't replace you. *Yet.*"

For a moment it appears as if Dorsky is going to rise

to that threat with anger.

Bronko's eyes flash hellfire at him.

Dorsky looks away.

Bronko nods. "You sort my kitchen out pronto and then you get the hell back to work. We're on the clock."

Dorsky levels his eyes with his executive chef.

He nods.

Bronko waits.

"Yes, Chef," Dorsky finally says.

"Okay, then."

"What about newbies?" Rollo asks in his thick accent.

Bronko looks back at Darren and Lena.

His expression is almost sad.

"They ain't newbies anymore," he says. "They're crew."

Darren is still too stunned to even process that, but Lena's own expression deepens into something almost fearful.

They all hear the clacking before they hear Jett's voice rise from the hallway.

"Byron! Byron!"

She pushes her way through the line cooks with surprising strength and ferocity.

"They're here!" she announces. "*It's* here. *It* and *they* are here!"

"Of course they are," Bronko says, more to himself than anyone else in the kitchen. "Thank you, Jett. I'll meet you in receiving, directly."

Jett nods spastically before turning and clacking away again.

Everyone is looking to him expectantly, many of them with confusion in their eyes. Bronko doesn't respond; he only walks over to one of the deep freezes, casually, in no rush.

As the rest of the staff watches, he fills one of their largest mixing bowls with ice, then carries it over to the station beside where Darren is standing.

When he tries to take the limb from the younger chef, Darren's grip only intensifies. His eyes widen.

Bronko's voice is gentler than it's yet been when he says, "You did good lookin' after this for the man, son, but let me go ahead and unburden you now. C'mon. It's okay."

Darren nods, beginning to snap back into the regular flow of things.

Bronko takes Ritter's arm and carefully packs it into the bowl of ice.

"Boss, what was she talking about?" Dorsky asks carefully. "Jett?"

Bronko doesn't answer at first. Instead he walks over to Pacific and gingerly plucks the joint from the kid's fingertips. He brings it to his own lips and draws in a long stream of the sweetly acrid smoke, holding it for several seconds before exhaling smoothly and expertly.

"Our main course," he says through slightly tightened vocal cords. "It has arrived."

With that Bronko exits the kitchen.

Darren looks down at Lena, still cradling a near-comatose Ritter in her arms.

She answers the confusion on his face with a shake of her head.

Lena looks at the regular cooks for some indication of what's about to happen and/or why it seems such an ominous event.

From the looks on their faces and the way they're reacting with one another, none of them appear to know what's going on either.

From what she's seen of this place so far, Lena can't imagine that's a good sign.

MAIN COURSE

"I am really terribly sorry for the delay, Mister Allensworth," Jett says to the nondescript man in the black Adidas running suit.

It's her third apology in the last ten minutes.

"Really, Miss Hollinshead, not a problem."

One could argue, and more than one at Sin du Jour has, that Allensworth looks so much like a government spook he doesn't look like one at all. They've never once seen him in a three-piece suit; no shiny wingtips, dark sunglasses, or pigtailed earpiece affixed to his skull.

They're standing in the company's receiving bay, a blank concrete space in the back of the building where they take large deliveries. There's a single loading dock, currently occupied by a cargo van as nondescript as Allensworth himself. Its rear doors are closed, its windows blackened to absolute pitch.

Thus far Allensworth is the only occupant to have disembarked.

"I want to assure you, sir, that the company is sparing no effort or resource in the planning and execution of this event. We're taking its importance and impact to heart. The lighting design my team is constructing alone will—"

"I don't doubt it will be tasteful and occasion-appropriate, Miss Hollinshead. We've retained Sin du Jour for more decades than I've been with the agency. You've never let us down before."

"Oh, and we will continue that tradition on my watch. Mine and Chef Luck's, of course."

"Of course."

"Speak of the devil and so on and so fuckin' forth," Bronko says from the receiving bay entrance.

Allensworth strides forward, smiling cordially and extending a hand. "You're not the devil, Bronko. You lack the Tyrone Power–like profile."

"I guess you'd know," Bronko says as he shakes the hand of a man he's always been convinced could tell you exactly where and what year cyborg Hitler was finally killed.

"You having problems today?" Allensworth asks.

"Nope. Business as usual. Which is to say our only god is chaos."

"I'll tell you, it's interesting you chose that metaphor."

"Why's that?"

Allensworth slips two fingers into his smiling maw and whistles sharply around them.

The back doors of the cargo van swing open on cue. Two large figures emerge from the darkness, both of them covered head to toe in what looks like modern tactical armor fashioned from obsidian rock. They each wear a draped hood like that of a medieval executioner, covered in arcane runes of a type that has remained undiscovered by human archaeology.

In one gloved hand each holds a small, unadorned scepter. Their free hands reach inside the cargo van and grip an unseen object. When they draw it forth it's a gargantuan domed serving platter, so large it could conceal a Shetland pony, resting atop a dais on wheels.

"It doesn't require refrigeration?" Bronko asks darkly, as if he already knows the answer and doesn't like it one bit.

"I'd advise you to keep this particular protein fresh for as long as possible. Don't worry; I'm providing you with a full dossier."

The attendants wheel the dais across the receiving bay until it rests less than six feet from Bronko. They abruptly swing the scepters in their hands, and each extends telescopically into a four-foot staff.

Bronko doesn't even flinch.

They slide each pole through a ring worked into the base of either side of the platter's domed lid.

They wait.

"Well?" Bronko asks, trying to conceal his simultaneous impatience and hesitation.

Allensworth, still smiling, flicks his chin toward the back of the receiving bay.

Bronko looks over his shoulder to see the bulk of his staff filling the receiving bay entrance. Every pair of eyes is watching the domed platter intently.

Frowning, he turns back to Allensworth and folds his arms across his chest, giving the man the slightest of nods.

Allensworth motions to the ghastly attendants.

The light spills out before any of them have seen the first sign of it. Later they'll describe it as white light, ghostly white, despite the truth that it has no real color. But whether the light touches him or her individually or not, simply being exposed to its presence tightens the chest and grips the mind of every staff member present.

The attendants lift the domed lid completely and each take two steps back, lowering it behind the platter on the dais.

There isn't a single grain of doubt in a single one of their minds as to what they're looking at, despite its lack of resemblance to anything they've ever seen depicted in human art over the last two thousand years.

It's an angel.

It is a genuine, living, fallen-to-Earth angel of God.

"We rigged up a binding spell to keep the angel on the trolley there, but your people can pass back and forth through it with no problem. It's new. I mean, it's old, ancient actually, but . . . well, you get it."

The man is speaking so casually, as if this were the most normal exchange in the world to be having in the loading dock of a New York City catering company.

"We'll expect you to use every part during service, of course," Allensworth says casually.

The staff mobbing the receiving bay entrance look at each other, the reality hitting them like a brick wrapped in horror.

Bronko simply nods again, his expression hard but undisturbed.

"You should feel honored, Bronko. Human hands have never dressed such a specimen before. This event represents a lot of firsts. For all of us."

Most of the angel's body is obscured by the epic wingspan curled around its form, but a sleek, hairless head rises above one feathery fold.

Bronko's gaze meets a large oval eye as black as the heavens before they were touched by the spark of creation.

"Bronk?" Allensworth asks. "Are we all good?"

Bronko is the furthest from "good" any mortal man has ever been.

"Yeah," he says. "We're good."

PART II

TEST KITCHEN

SECOND INTERVIEW

"It helps if you think of it kind of, like, the National Geographic channel," Bronko says.

Lena and Darren are sitting in his office. Lena is robotically working her way through a second mug of the coffee spiked with cognac Chef Luck offered them both after ordering them into the chairs arranged in front of his desk. Darren is still nursing his first and untouched mugful, looking as pensive as an altar boy in a confessional line.

"National . . . what?" Lena asks Chef in the breathless wake of a long gulp.

"You know, you watch the National Geographic channel and you see maybe some gigantic spider from the Amazon, and it ain't anything you ever imagine existed in the world. It looks like something from science fiction. But it doesn't throw your whole self into upheaval, you know? You accept it. It isn't unnatural, just unexpected. The things you've seen today are kind of like that. It helps if you put it all into context, I find."

Darren actually nods at this.

Lena's head snaps around to shoot him a look that could wilt petals made of steel.

He looks back at her and shrugs, still wide-eyed.

Lena tips the mug in her hand and drinks down the last few ounces of booze-infused Colombian roast. She exhales like a drowning woman breaking the surface of the water.

Then she stares at Bronko.

She says: "What . . . the *fuck* . . . are you talking about, Chef?" Each of her next words rises progressively in volume and intensity. "Are you out of your mind? Is everyone here fucking whacked in the head? Is this some kind of sick fucking rib on us or something?"

"Lena!" Darren hisses at her.

"No, fuck that! I had to field-dress a man's stump like we just drove over a motherfucking I.E.D. But it wasn't a roadside detonation; it was a monster that came out of a jar in the forbidden pantry from Hell! And then . . . and then . . . one of the Men in Black delivers a . . . a . . ."

"Angel," Bronko says deliberately.

That word spoken aloud and with conviction seems to deflate Lena's rage immediately.

It's replaced by a deep sulk.

"Bullshit," she mutters into her cup.

Bronko stands, pushing his chair away and striding slowly around his desk. He sits on its edge between them, folding his thick arms over his thicker chest, and looks down on them like the goodhearted high school principal trying to reach a pair of troublemaking freshmen.

"What I'm going to tell you now I don't generally share with temps. You can understand that, I'm sure."

Darren begins to nod.

Then, casting a glance at Lena, he thinks better of it.

Lena continues to stare at Chef with laser focus.

"Sin du Jour has a single client. It has since . . . well, before I became executive chef. That client is a branch of the United States government. However, it ain't any branch you'll ever hear about on CNN or read about on Twitter or whatever-the-hell. It's a branch that deals with . . . it's like a diplomatic service, except it works with things . . . folks . . . like you saw today."

"Angels and monsters in jars?"

"No. Uh, the thing in the jar is food."

"And the angel is too?"

"I'd . . . we've never seen anything like that before today, so I don't know. I guess so."

"It's real?" Darren asks, childlike. "That was really an angel?"

"Yes, son. It's real."

"Who or what *eats* angels?" Lena demands.

Bronko sighs. He squeezes the bridge of his nose between his thumb and forefinger as if to tourniquet a gushing wound.

"Now, this is for lack of a better term. All right? Try to keep a lid on the connotations it, you know, brings to mind."

They both wait.

"Demons," Bronko says, immediately clearing his throat in the wake of the word.

Lena bolts then. She practically leaps from her chair and almost springboards over its back. She's crossed the room and made it to the door in record time.

When she opens it, Lena finds the entire staff of Sin du Jour standing out in the hall, staring at her.

She closes the door just as quickly.

"Lena," Bronko urges gently, "let me finish before you go making up your mind, okay? Please?"

Her heart and brain are racing each other on five-hundred-mile-an-hour rails.

"Please," Chef repeats more firmly.

Lena eases back over to her chair, although it's obvious her brain is still working overtime.

"There are groups . . . races . . . of folks you'd only know from stories. They exist, they *ain't* from stories, and they live and work and . . . they're just folks, here, among us. Government knows about it, keeps it under wraps. They negotiate with 'em to keep the secret, keep the peace. It's like a diplomatic agency. It's just one you don't hear about, because that's the whole point. We contract with them."

"And demons—"

"Are one of those groups."

"Like, from Hell?"

"Sometimes. And sometimes from Park Avenue."

"And you feed them?"

"We cater events for Uncle Sam. The one we're prepping is a banquet for two rival clans who just signed some big treaty. This shindig is to help seal the deal. It's important. It helps stop a war that could spill onto human streets. It's a good thing, believe it or not."

"Two clans of demons."

"Yes."

"What were we prepping?" Darren asks. "The apps? I'd never tasted anything like that before."

Bronko grins.

"And you never will. Once you get past the peculiars of our clientele, you begin to see a whole new culinary world open up right in front of you. We work with products and ingredients you can't even conceive of, kids. Truly amazing things."

"Like angels," Lena says flatly.

Bronko's grin conveys something between rueful and sad.

"I told you. Before today . . . I couldn't have told you

for sure they existed."

"Well, they do. You have one in your kitchen, Chef. And our own government apparently expects you to kill it and serve it. To a clan of demons."

"Two clans," Darren corrects her.

"Darren, for fuck's sake!"

"Look, y'all can go if you want."

"I don't believe that," Lena says.

"Why not?" Darren asks, looking at her, then up at Bronko.

"You just told us this epic secret the government is keeping and we can just leave knowing it?"

Bronko nods.

"How?"

He shrugs. "Who are you going to tell? And what are you going to say? That there's a catering outfit in New York City serving angel stew to demons?"

"Fine. Then I'm leaving."

Bronko only nods again.

"Come on," she says to Darren, already heading for the door.

"I'm—"

Darren hesitates.

She looks down at him.

"I'm going to hang out a while, El."

"What?"

"It was an angel. A real angel! You want to just leave?"

"Fuck, yes!"

Darren nods.

He finally takes a sip from his mug.

"Okay, then. Go ahead. But I'm staying."

"Darren!"

"I'm staying!" he shouts back at her with equal volume, equal timbre.

It's very un-Darren-like.

"Sweetie? They are going to kill that thing and cook it! And serve it to minions of Hell! Literally!"

"Maybe not," Darren says resolutely, and then he turns and looks pointedly at Chef Luck.

"Are you, Chef?" Darren asks. "Are you really going to . . . do that?"

"I don't know, son," Bronko answers, and even Lena can't deny the sincerity and tragedy in his voice.

Darren nods.

He looks up at Lena.

"I'm staying," he says with finality.

Lena practically vibrates.

But she's not going to leave a man behind.

In the end, all she does is push a single word through her teeth.

"Fine."

"You can go if you want," Darren assures her. "It's

okay. I'll understand."

She shakes her head.

Lena knows if she tries to say any more she'll scream it.

But she doesn't move.

"You're staying too, then?" Bronko asks. "For now, anyway?"

Lena nods stiffly.

Bronko grins anew. "All right, then. You're both hired, for real this time."

It takes a few seconds before Lena can be sure of her tone.

Then she says, "So what are you going to do, Chef?"

"About the angel," Darren adds.

"Yeah. About that. What are you going to do if you're not just going to butcher it?"

Bronko leans back in his chair.

"Well, now . . ."

STAFF VOTE

The line crew of Sin du Jour—five of them—all stand against the ranges in the back of the kitchen.

Tag Dorsky, their leader and sous-chef, is reclining against a flattop in the middle of the row, arms crossed, looking like a pretender to some imaginary throne.

Chef Luck, Darren and Lena at his flanks, gestures down the line.

"Dorsky you know. The circus bear standing next to him is Rollo. Then you've got Chevet there in the Chef Boyardee toque, but don't let that fool you. He earned a Michelin star when he was working in straight joints. Tenryu, the boys call him the Professor, probably just to be racist. And then James on the end there."

James smiles genuinely and waves at them both.

He's the only one.

"Good to meet you for real this time," he says with a slight Senegalese accent.

"So what's up, Chef?" Dorsky asks. "I know the newbies caused a little fracas in the pantry, but we've got a big event to prep for here. Bigger than we thought, I'd say."

"We've got a vote to take," Chef Luck announces. "Cooking for demons is one thing. That's business, and nomenclature aside we've probably done events for worse. We've also been asked to serve some strange product, maybe even product that walked a fine line. But this . . . is different. And we all know it. And it crosses a line. I don't believe a kitchen is a democracy, but all the same I'm not ordering anyone across that line."

"So what are we voting on?" Dorsky asks.

"We're voting on whether or not to service the client's request."

"And what if we don't? We can't walk on the gig. We don't work for the fucking Shriners here, Chef. They hold us accountable. You know that."

"They do, which is why we're not walking on the gig. What we will do is serve a substitute for our main entrée."

"They've agreed to that?"

"No, Dorsky, they haven't."

"So you want us to vote to fuck over a conclave of warring demon clans and the government? I mean, the actual government."

"I'm not telling anyone how to vote. And I'm not voting. I'm abstaining here. This is the line's decision. And anyone not happy with the vote can walk if they choose. But this is how it's going to be."

Dorsky looks over the faces of the rest of the cooks,

then back at Bronko.

"You put me in charge of the line," Dorsky says. "It's my job to speak for it. And I say we're doing the damn job. We all know who our clients are here."

The rest of the cooks nod in agreement.

Except for James.

"Sorry, man," he says. "I can't be down for this one."

Dorsky doesn't even attempt to mask his anger and disdain.

"What the hell?"

"No one seems to want to say the words, so I will. They want us to kill an angel of God. That's what we have here. I won't do that. I could never go home again."

Dorsky rolls his eyes. "Jesus."

"Exactly," James says with conviction.

"Fine! That's Four-to-one for doing the job. Walk if you want, James. Those five rug rats of yours will appreciate it, I'm sure."

Lena cuts in: "It's four-to-three, actually."

All heads turn to her, many as if seeing her for the first time.

"Darren and I vote no. Right?"

Darren nods, trying very hard not to meet any of the line's gazes.

"Where's Nikki?" Chef Luck asks the room.

"Who knows?" Dorsky answers, irritated. "Who

cares? The pastry puff will vote for clemency just to stick it up the line's ass."

"You mean your ass," James corrects him.

"Don't fucking push me, dude."

"All right, so assume her vote is negative," Chef says. "That splits it dead even."

Dorsky explodes. "Whoa! Why do the newbies even get a vote?"

"They're hires now."

"All due respect, Chef, I call it two against and four to do our damn jobs. Their votes shouldn't mean dick."

Lena shakes her head, grinning darkly. "Unbelievable."

Dorsky looks directly at her for the first time. "Do you have something to say to me?"

"I'm in a kitchen that cooks for fucking demons and it's the same goddamn bullies running it you find on the line in Manhattan. Nothing changes."

"Lena!" Darren warns her quietly.

"No, fuck that," she says. "It's a tied vote. And I don't even care anyway because no one's killing or serving whatever that thing is we saw while I'm around. It's not happening. Deal with it, big man."

Dorsky smiles.

It's a joyless expression.

"You want to be staff?" he asks Lena. "You want to

be on the line? Okay, girl. There's a real easy way to settle shit like this in our kitchen. It's a tradition that goes back a ways. It's a guaranteed dispute settler."

"Dorsky," Bronko warns. "We got enough shit going on right now."

"You're abstaining, Chef. Remember?"

"What is it?" Lena asks wryly. "Pissing for distance? Because I'm surprisingly good at that."

"No," Dorsky says, still smiling. "But you will drop some body fluids. I guarantee you that, too."

THE BAKER

The main dry storage room of Sin du Jour is filled with a light unseen on Earth since a time of abject innocence.

And that was long ago, indeed.

Nikki Glowin, flour shrapnel sprinkled among the many vintage victory rolls binding her hair, pulls open the heavy storage room door and is briefly blinded by it.

"What the hell, man—"

The initial shock of the light fades, and with it goes her next words as her eyes adjust to the light's source.

The angel is sprawled atop a large rolling cart, held there by a binding spell more powerful than anything unleashed in the human world since a time immediately following abject innocence, when chaos unburdened by any rational thought reigned.

Naked and unashamed, it's a creature neither male nor female. Its bipedal form is where its resemblance to any human being ends, in fact. It's more like a featherless bird in body, with an elongated face, no nose, not even slits, and on each side of its skull a large, glassy oval swirling with dark tones serving as its eyes. Its limbs are longer and slimmer, skin a pale gray, the digits of its hands and feet three-pronged and pinned with yellow talons.

Nikki's eyes take all of those features in last.

At first there's nothing but its wings.

They are less like a bird's and more like the fleshy form to which they are attached. Each one is shaped as a perfect triangle, more silken and illusory than dense with feathers and sinew, although there are feathers. They wilt and shudder around its body with each breath.

They're the source of the unearthly light.

Nikki involuntarily rubs her right bicep, smearing yet more flour over the weeping angel tattooed there in vivid colors.

"Are you—?" she begins, then stops.

The angel cocks its head in her general direction.

It doesn't speak.

Nikki is suddenly very aware of her stained, flour-covered apron, and of the scantily clad pinup girl emblazoned on it beneath those stains and that flour.

She feels like a dirty peasant standing in the court of royalty.

She clears her throat and, as she often does, especially in situations made of uncertainty, says the first thing that comes to mind.

"Can I . . . bring you a cupcake?"

Again, the angel cocks its head.

SECOND BLOOD

"You're not actually going to do this, are you?"

"You wanted to stay."

Lena and Darren are standing in the courtyard at the center of Sin du Jour headquarters. It's walled with bricks that appear to be more red dust than solid matter. The stone fountain in the middle of the open space hasn't tasted water in a century or more.

"We can leave if you want," Darren tells her.

She flashes him what only Darren recognizes as her "Lena" look.

"They're *not* killing . . . whatever that is. I won't allow it."

"The angel."

"Whatever!"

Back in the kitchen Chef Luck silently selected two wicked-looking paring knives and led the entire staff outside. Now he's standing in the middle of the courtyard, flipping them both in his hands, the size of which make the blades look even smaller.

The busboys (one of whom is in his seventies) are

sitting in foldout concert chairs beside the fountain. They're passing an expertly rolled joint back and forth.

"Chef's dispute?" the younger one Chef earlier referred to as "Pacific" asks through a wraith made of smoke.

Chef Luck nods.

"Sick," Pacific says, as excited as one can be after a dozen tokes of top-quality sativa.

"*Que es?*" Mr. Mirabal, the oldest busboy in New York, asks him.

Pacific curls a fist and swipes it in front of him, making swashbuckling sound effects with his mouth.

His elderly companion nods, wide-eyed. "Oh."

Chef Luck hands one of the paring knives to Lena, the other to Dorsky, who takes it with easy familiarity and a grin.

Bronko addresses the courtyard: "The rules are simple, but I'd pay attention were I a newcomer to such things. No puncturing, no stabbing. Slashing only. You keep it confined to the torso, nothing above the shoulders or below the waist. It's a sight to second blood. You draw your fellow chef's blood twice and you win. A drop counts, so keep it as civil as a knife fight can be. Tarr here wins, her newbie vote counts, so does Vargas's there. Dorsky wins, newbies don't get a vote, majority rules . . . we serve angel at the gig. Everyone agreed?"

Dorksy and the staff all nod, everyone grinning, save for James.

But he's standing with them, regardless.

Lena turns the knife over and over in her hand, staring down at it as if its thick handle and steel blade were the flesh and bones of a fallen friend.

She looks up at Chef and nods.

Perhaps because no one else is standing with him, Bronko joins Darren on the opposite side of the courtyard from the rest of the crew.

Lena moves away from them toward the courtyard center.

"Chef, why are you letting them do this?" Darren asks, desperate.

Bronko folds his arms over his chest, not looking at the younger chef. "A kitchen like ours, working so close to the kind of action most people only read about in fuckin' Harry Potter or some shit, things like this tend to get more elevated than usual. As you've seen. If I didn't let you kids play the part now and then, you'd lose your shit."

"What if someone gets killed?" Darren pleads.

Bronko shrugs. "I got as many magicians working for me as chefs. Short of someone's head coming off there's never been something we couldn't fix. It'll be fine, son. I'm more worried about their egos than their bodies."

Darren can't think of anything else to say, but the twisted expression on his face speaks volumes.

Bronko finally looks down at him, sees it.

"She doesn't have to do it," Bronko tells him.

Darren frowns. "Lena doesn't know how to back down."

Dorsky is already hunched over, arms curled and leading with his knife hand.

He's not only ready for a fight.

He's savoring it.

Lena, on the other hand, looks like she's attending a funeral.

Dorsky begins circling her. Lena doesn't mirror his movements. She stays planted in one spot, only rotating her body so that she's always facing in his direction. Her arms remain at her sides, passively, although if you examined her knife hand closely you'd see she's almost strangling the grip of the paring blade.

Dorsky swipes his blade a few inches shy of her a few times, just trying to scare her.

Lena doesn't scare.

She doesn't move either.

The grin on his face fades somewhat.

Suddenly he leaps forward in earnest, slashing at her left breast.

Lena calmly but with surprising speed and grace of

movement sidesteps the strike. She reaches up and grabs his extended arm, yanking it with all of her strength and sending him stumbling forward off-balance. As he does, Lena strips the edge of her paring knife across his forearm and steps away.

When Dorsky recovers and spins around she's out of arm's reach.

He's breathing heavy and bleeding from a shallow cut a few inches from his knife hand.

"First blood!" Chef Luck announces.

"Goddamn!" Pacific calls from his chair, coughing on a lungful of smoke as he begins to applaud and laugh.

Mr. Mirabal joins him. "Good for you, mami! You go!"

The rest of the kitchen crew is speechless.

They're also too surprised and distracted to notice James finally grinning.

Dorsky raises his arm and examines the cut.

He looks across the courtyard at her, still breathing hard.

"They teaching that in culinary school now?" Dorsky asks.

"I didn't go to culinary school."

"Yeah? So where'd you learn to cook?"

"The same place I learned to fight. In the army."

Dorsky's expression is now the exact opposite of a

grin.

"Shit."

Lena nods. "Yeah."

He takes a deep, pensive breath and then explodes toward her once again, slashing wildly.

Lena backs away from his attack, staying ahead of the knife, looking for her opening. Her close-quarters combat instructor during IET had been another female enlisted. She understood what it is to constantly face opponents of superior size and strength. One day she'd pulled Lena aside to give her this piece of advice: "Make yourself even smaller, as small as you can, until it's time to make yourself big and strike."

Lena stops backing up, allowing Dorsky's advance to meet her. She reverses her grip on the knife as she ducks quickly under Dorsky's attacking arm, almost crouching all the way to the cobbled ground. Dorsky practically trips over her, losing his concentration for a split second.

It's a long enough span of time to allow Lena to uncoil and slash his armpit as she does.

"Fucking shit!" Dorsky cries out in pain, nearly stabbing himself as he presses his knife-cradling fist into the sudden wound.

"That's it!" Chef Luck proclaims. "That's second blood. It's over. Newbies' votes stand. We figure out a plan B."

Lena drops her knife, raising both of her hands in compliance. She's breathing heavily too now, mostly from nerves.

Dorsky, however, doesn't seem to hear his executive chef.

"Fucking bitch!" he growls, rushing Lena anew, still holding his knife.

"Hey!" Darren cries out.

Lena's eyes go wide. She glances briefly down at the knife on the cobbles, but it's too late. Dorsky slashes wildly at her. She turns and dashes across the courtyard with him at her heels.

Until he's met by Bronko.

The chef suddenly has Dorsky in a half nelson, holding both of his arms at bay and twisting the man's body until his sous-chef is forced to one knee.

Dorsky struggles, and he's a big, powerful man, younger than Luck, but those advanced years and the work they've contained have only forged Bronko's muscles into unseen iron.

"You keep it up," he breathes heavily into Dorsky's ear, "I'll not only fire you, I'll bust your fucking skull open before I kick your ass out the door. You get me?"

Dorsky nods.

He heard that.

Bronko releases his grip on the younger chef and

stands, turning to face the rest of the crew.

"Can we get back to cooking now?"

No one answers, but it's obvious no one will dare argue either.

"Good. Get your asses back in that kitchen."

He walks over to Lena as the rest of them file back inside the building.

"You okay?"

She nods. "He must be a really talented chef."

"Dorsky? He's got the right temperament for this particular job. Most of the time."

"Then I guess I don't," Lena says harshly.

Bronko grins. "All evidence to the contrary, kid."

Darren has joined them. "Chef?"

"Yeah, Vargas?"

"What are we going to do now? If we're not . . . if we're not serving the angel."

Bronko nods. "We're going to consult the expert."

As Lena and Darren, their confusion obvious, follow him back inside Sin du Jour, the busboys share a final toke.

"That was some crazy shit," Pacific comments idly. "Even for this place."

Mr. Mirabal nods. He coughs violently, then presses his air tube into both nostrils with his thumb and inhales through his nose.

"Your shit's getting stronger too," he says.

Pacific laughs. "Yeah, well. I don't want us building up a tolerance. You know?"

SHE TALKS TO ANGELS

The old woman isn't entirely human.

Lena can see Darren is ignoring it, looking away like someone trying not to focus on the unexpected physical deformity of a person they've just met, but Lena has never been able to ignore any reality with which she's faced.

The obvious fact is the old woman, or mostly woman, is not deformed.

She's a hybrid of human being and something else.

Her features are just a little off. Her eyes and ears and nose and mouth—they're all present, but spaced differently than an average person's. And there's a perfect uniformity to it all that defies aberration or deformity.

Her skin is also tinted green.

Bronko has escorted them to a small space in the very back corner of the kitchen level, far removed from everything else.

"You might say she's Sin du Jour's taster," he explains briefly, distractedly. "Some of our recipes are centuries old, some have never been made by . . . well, people.

Boosha's . . . been around."

It smells of iodine and herbs and is cluttered with aging leather-bound volumes and murky bottles. It's as if someone has merged a hundred-year-old spice rack with an even more ancient library.

Bronko introduces them. "Boosha, this is Lena, this is Darren, together they fight crime, and they're also our new line cooks."

Boosha nods uninterestedly. She has her face buried in an old tome set on a pedestal. Lena can make out arcane and horrifying illustrations on its vellum pages.

"Kids, this is Boosha."

The not-entirely-an-old-woman snorts a laugh through her nostrils.

The slightly mangy Shih Tzu at her feet won't stop barking around a gnawed chicken bone.

Lena kneels and scratches behind his ears with both hands.

"What's his name?" she asks.

"Dog," Boosha informs her distractedly.

Lena frowns. "That's not much of a name."

"Found him in alley scratching on door yesterday. Is what his collar says."

"Oh."

Bronko interjects, "You going to pretend like you don't already know and make me ask?"

"Angel," Boosha says casually. "Is very rare."

"No shit, Boosh."

For the first time she looks up, sharply, and hisses at him.

"Language!" she snaps.

"Sorry."

Boosha's accent sounds Eastern European to Lena and Darren and is nothing any Eastern European would recognize.

"You know what they want us to do?" Bronko asks her.

She nods. "And you will not."

"And we will not. If we can get away with it, that is."

"Of course."

"Will they recognize the taste? Will they know it or not know it automatically?"

Boosha taps the current page in the book she's been perusing.

"Oexial and Vig'nerash are clans coming together at banquet. Oexial is oldest demon clan. I have little Oexial in me myself. Vig'nerash is fiery young ones. Is possible Oexial elders remember taste, but is not likely. Last angel to be served to demons was more years ago than your ancestors have seen. Most who would be old enough to remember taste of angel are dead now."

"Demons can die?" Darren asks, perpetually in awe at

this point.

"Everything dies, little one," Boosha informs him kindly.

"So if we know what angel tastes like we can probably fake it," Bronko says, more to himself than any of them.

"All things are possible," Boosha muses. "Illusion is often easiest."

Nikki wheels in the subdued angel, who is cradling a half-eaten cupcake between its strange hands.

"You wanted to see us, boss?" she says.

Bronko smiles. "My new angel-sitter."

"Yeah, I have another skill. Who knew?"

Bronko points at her. "Lena, Darren, this is our resident pastry chef, Nikki."

Nikki smiles at the newbies. "Helluva first day, huh?"

"Yeah. Hi," is all Lena offers.

Darren is still shell-shocked by the sight of the angel.

Lena elbows him.

"Oh." He looks up at Nikki. "Uh, nice to meet you. I like your hair."

"Thanks, hon."

"Can you communicate with it?" Bronko asks his matronly taster.

"It?"

"Her. Him. Whatever."

"Angel is neither man nor woman. Men and women

came later."

"Our *guest,*" Bronko restates. "Can you speak to them?"

Boosha shakes her head. "Is oldest sound."

"You mean 'language.'"

"No," she says impatiently. "Is oldest sound."

"Okay, fine. So you can't."

"No."

"Can it understand us?"

Boosha shrugs. "Intention, perhaps. Human spirit, human emotion. Not human words."

"Well, I have a very specific request, so that's gonna be tough."

Dog chooses that moment to start barking again.

Bronko, his temples already threatening to throb off his skull, is ready to yell at the stray to shut up.

Instead the angel seems to do it for him.

Boosha is right: it's not a language as any of them understand the concept. It's sound, and such a sound has never touched their ears. It should be a shriek, a horrifying, screeching, guttural noise, but even as they're all aware of what it should be, what it sounds like is music. It's almost like birdsong piped directly into their cerebral cortex.

None of them speak.

Dog barks again.

The angel's shriek-song answers him.

They're looking directly at each other, and it becomes clear, no denying it, that they're having a conversation.

Lena tries to, anyway. "Oh, come on. They're not—"

"Dog understands angel," Boosha says. "Angel understands dog. Animals are closer to God in such a way."

"How do you know?" Lena asks, ever the skeptic.

"I understand dog," she says simply.

"Bullshit."

"Why do you think the damn dog is back here?" Bronko snaps at Lena, moving on before she can reply. "We need its help. The angel's."

Dog turns his head and barks at Boosha.

"Angel's name is Ramiel," she explains.

Bronko looks directly into the angel's face for the first time. "Ramiel. No one here wants to hurt you. But we can't just refuse to do this. It puts all of my people in danger. And if we do refuse, they'll just get someone else. So, I need your help."

Boosha gathers her skirts and, with a grunt, crouches down to whisper into the Shih Tzu's ear.

Dog barks sporadically, like canine Morse code, in between the old crone's whispers.

Ramiel's response is the sound of diamonds scratching glass.

Dog listens, then translates with a few yaps.

Boosha looks up at Bronko.

"What help do you require?"

Bronko looks at Darren, Lena, and Nikki heavily.

"We need to know what angels taste like."

After Boosha and Dog have conveyed the request to Ramiel, the angel turns its volcanic glass eyes on Bronko.

Ramiel extends a hand toward him.

Again, diamonds scratching glass followed by a Shih Tzu's yapping.

"Ramiel says for you to take hand," Boosha explains.

"Jesus," Lena says under her breath.

Bronko stares at the angel's proffered hand.

"He would've had a more elegant solution, I'm sure."

A POUND OF FLESH

Lena asks if they'll draw lots to decide who takes the angel's hand.

"No," Bronko says, a weighty pronouncement. "I put deciding whether or not to do this on you guys. This is on me. I'll do it."

He orders her, Darren, and Nikki out of Boosha's ramshackle apothecary.

Ramiel is resting on its hip atop an island prep station in the middle of the room. Bronko doesn't know how to read the emotions of an angel, and in truth he doesn't want to be able to do so in that moment.

Boosha does what an eternal grandmother always does.

She hovers.

Bronko has selected a ceramic meat cleaver. It's not nearly as heavy as steel, but the edge is far finer and sharper.

He trusts his strength to do the rest.

Bronko hefts the cleaver in his hand and moves to stand over the prep station.

Ramiel stretches its limb across the dense wood surface of a large cutting block.

An arm has never looked so much like a child's to Bronko, so slight and fragile, flesh so unmarred by the inevitable ugliness of life.

His stomach churns like a cauldron filled with acid and regret.

Ramiel shrieks softly.

Dog barks.

Bronko glances over at Boosha, who flicks her chin and informs him, casually, "Angel says this will leave mark."

Bronko brings his eyes back to the task before him.

He raises his executioner's arm.

He doesn't look up at Ramiel's face.

"No shit," he says flatly, and strikes.

The fine hatchet's edge swipes cleanly through divine flesh, no bone beneath it and that's something they'll all marvel at and endlessly question later. The blade embeds itself in the cutting block beneath the newly severed limb.

Ramiel makes not a sound.

Bronko screams.

He won't remember what, if any, images flashed before his mind's eye in that moment. Instead he'll describe the images conjured by its memory. It will be like both of your parents frowning deeply down on you, and feeling their eternal disappointment, knowing you will never rise above it and fully attain the love they once conveyed to you in every look and every gesture.

In the kitchen, the moment after the strike, it also makes him violently ill.

Bronko drops to one knee. His hand is still strangling the handle of the cleaver, the blade of which is still buried in the chopping block. His other hand grips the edge of the counter to steady and steel himself as the most intense nausea of his life assaults him in staggered, lapping waves.

It passes in moments that feel like months, and leaves behind a mercury switch that feels as if it will trigger projectile vomiting with the slightest movement.

Bronko doesn't move.

"I told you," Boosha says, her voice slightly more weighted with emotion than before. "It will leave mark."

Dog pads up beside where Bronko kneels.

The Shih Tzu places its chicken bone carefully on the floor and begins nuzzling Bronko's leg.

Above him, Bronko is touched by cool and warmth at the same time. A gentle, electric grip covers his fist and causes it to slip from the handle of the meat cleaver.

Suddenly, the sickness dissipates.

He stands, shakily but without heaving everything he's eaten since last night all over the kitchen.

Ramiel looks up at him from the station with unabashed sympathy.

The sight of the angel's face makes him want to cry.

Instead he looks away, at the cutting block. Ramiel's "blood," if it truly is that, looks like honey. Flecks of gold and white within its viscosity play in the light. There isn't very much of it either. Neither Ramiel's arm nor the angel's severed hand is bleeding. Neither of them wear gore nor twitch with pain.

Ramiel isn't even cradling its stump.

Which appears as though it is already healing.

"I'm sorry," Bronko exhales, hoarse and ragged, still not looking at the angel.

Ramiel makes a haunted-house-door creak of a sound.

Dog barks.

"He forgives you," Boosha says.

Bronko looks over at her, brow furrowed.

"I thought angels weren't boys or girls."

Boosha shakes her head. "Is not who angel meant."

"Oh."

As Bronko attempts to process that, along with the last few minutes of his life, Boosha picks up the angel's hand with a pair of ancient, torturous-looking tongs and places it in an ordinary everyday hotel pan, covering it with the corresponding lid.

She picks up the hotel pan and shoves it into Bronko's chest decisively.

"You take," she orders. "I see to angel. If you need help with flavor, come back."

Bronko nods dumbly, closing his large hands around the edges of the hotel pan.

Lena, Nikki, and Darren are waiting for him out in the hall.

"Jesus, Chef, are you okay?" Darren asks with more sympathy than horror, although it's present in his voice as well.

"Test kitchen," is all Bronko says.

They follow him.

Bronko has a handle on his psyche now. He disconnects from everything except the job. He treats the angel's hand like any product, Earthly or supernatural.

None of them want to watch him butcher the angel's flesh, but none of them, not even Darren, look away.

They all somehow know they need to support their chef in that moment.

The fillet between the forefinger and thumb is the most delicate and tender of meats. Bronko bisects it carefully. There's no visible sinew or tendon to clean or cut through; it is simply flesh.

Once the cut is ready, Bronko glazes a sauté pan with simple, everyday cooking spray; the can actually has dust on it from lack of use. No chef in his kitchen would normally use anything other than olive oil or butter, but Bronko doesn't want to taste anything except the angel's flesh.

They need to know exactly what its flavor says to the palate.

It takes him only a few minutes to work the appropriate amount of heat through the small fillet and put a light sear on its surfaces. Darren, Lena, and Nikki await the smell of it cooking eagerly, and with more than a little fear.

None of them comment on the scent that hits their nostrils; they only look at each other quizzically and uncertainly.

When Bronko is done, he puts the fillet on an appetizer plate and cuts it into four pieces.

"I'd like to say none of y'all have to do this," he tells them, "but you do. If we're going to pull this off, you do."

Nikki, more to have something to do and contribute and only slightly less because she's the eternal helper, retrieves and lays out four small forks in front of the plate.

Darren looks to Lena, as he often does.

She reaches up and squeezes his arm.

"All right, present arms," their chef instructs them.

They all pick up their forks.

They each skewer a piece of cooked angel flesh.

They each hold their bite under their noses.

Again, their eyes find each other's and exchange rank confusion.

They all taste angel flesh for the first and last time.

No one reacts visibly as they chew.

Neither do they react when they each swallow.

No one utters a single word for almost sixty full seconds afterward.

Bronko finally breaks the silence: "Well, who's going to be the one to say it?"

It's as if he's giving them permission, and all three of them seem to need it.

"Nuggies," Darren blurts out, and then almost covers his mouth in embarrassment.

They all nod.

Bronko heaviest of all.

"Nuggies," Lena seconds. "It tastes exactly like Chicken Nuggies from a fucking Henley's joint."

"I thought it smelled like fast food in here," Bronko says.

Nikki is more aghast than any of them. "I can't believe it. Chicken, sure. But . . . Chicken Nuggies. I just—"

"The consistency is completely different," Bronko says clinically, his wheels spinning.

Lena nods. "Yeah, it doesn't feel like a Nuggie in your mouth at all, but the taste is dead-on."

"Which means we can't actually just peel the breading off a bunch of Nuggies and serve them."

"No, Chef."

"No, Chef."

"No, Ch—" Nikki's tongue stumbles. "I just can't believe it! Chicken Nuggies?"

"Deal with it, Glowin," Bronko instructs her.

"Yes, Chef."

"I can go on the Internet," Darren offers. "Try to find the recipe?"

Bronko nods.

Then he looks at Lena.

"Most important rule of working here," he tells her. "Just when you think you've got a handle on how fucking sick the universe's sense of humor is, it goes and tells you an even dirtier joke."

Lena doesn't know whether to laugh or cry.

Bronko walks over to the nearest sink and spits.

"Fuckin' Nuggies," he mutters. "I hate Henley's."

MARCHING ORDERS

Darren follows Bronko down a narrow and rusted stairwell between stripped-paint walls. They've left the kitchens and magazine-cover façade of Sin du Jour far behind and are now descending the sublevels beneath the old brick building.

Having left Lena with Nikki to work on the rest of their substitute menu for the demon banquet, Bronko felt Darren should stay by the chef's side until, as he puts it, Darren "shakes off that little-lost-puppy vibe."

"I know it's not really my place, Chef," Darren says nervously, "but isn't this kind of, like, extreme?"

"It's not 'like' extreme. It *is* extreme. But we don't have a choice."

They've spent the rest of the afternoon and evening cooking test versions of imitation angel. Darren pulled dozens of homebrewed and so-called hacked recipes for Henley's signature Chicken Nuggies off as many websites. They are all relatively similar in terms of ingredients, varying only in proportions.

None of them nail the taste of the world-famous fast-food concoction.

"There's some kinda chemical differential. Some preservative or pesticide or some shit, probably proprietary. Without it, the taste is always going to be off. We need to know what it is, that's all there is to it. We're already working at a handicap, assuming we can pass off some free-range regular-ass protein for a fucking divine creation of the Lord Itself."

"But can they really do something like that? Your . . . the receiving guys?"

"Receiving *folks,* if you please. Kid, most restaurants and catering services, their stocking and receiving departments' job is to hit up the farmers' market every morning. Sin du Jour employs a slightly different set for our needs. This'll be like a vacation for 'em. You'll see."

The stairwell ends with a cast-iron door that might've been forged to withstand an atomic blast. Bronko easily yanks back its latch and kicks it open, as if he's performed the action a million times before.

Darren half expects a steaming and dripping boiler room straight out of some bargain-bin 1980s horror movie. Instead the door groans open onto a simple, well-kept hallway. The walls are painted a yellow not seen since AstroTurf was fashionable, and it's faded with age, but otherwise the sight is totally benign.

There's also music.

The joyful agony of Louis Armstrong's immortal trumpet winds throughout the hall.

"Satchmo," Bronko comments idly. "My man."

They follow the gravel-filled soul of the singer's voice down the hallway, passing doors burdened with heavy locks that both look to be more secure replacements for whatever particle board was originally there. The hall ends under a sign made of strips of beige masking tape adhered to the wall above the awning. STOCKING & RECEIVING has been scrawled on the rows of tape in thick black marker by an unconcerned hand.

Darren squints up at the makeshift sign, confused, then Bronko taps him lightly on the chest and motions him through the awning.

It opens into a large concrete space that might have resembled a maniac's kill room if it weren't plastered with posters promoting decades-old martial arts tournaments, awful circa-1990s rock bands, vintage muscle cars, and one oddly elegant and out-of-place Jean-Léon Gérôme print. There are foam practice mats covering much of the floor, along with some busted Goodwill furniture lining the walls. The rest is relatively Spartan.

The four members of Sin du Jour's mysterious and concealed department Darren met earlier are all here. The giant, Hara, and the woman even more solidly built than Lena who Darren remembers as Cindy (he has always been good with names, as he is terrified of forgetting anyone's and thus offending them and embarrassing himself) are taking turns hurling knives at what looks like a giant dart board.

They aren't cooking knives, either.

These are knives forged for combat.

The little one, the weasel-looking man who doesn't seem to fit—Moon—is reclining on a sofa that's bleeding insulation in several places. He's cramming potato chips into his mouth from a half-eaten bag while watching something unseen on his iPhone and listening to it through a pair of earbuds.

Ritter is sitting behind a folding card table. At first Darren doesn't even take notice of it, then it hits him suddenly, causing his legs to lock midstride.

Ritter is sitting behind a folding card table, and he possesses two intact, fully functioning arms.

His left arm is folded above his head, hand twined in his hair as if ordered there by a police officer. His right arm, the arm Darren cradled that very morning after watching it severed from the rest of Ritter's body, is stretched across the table. It's once more attached to him.

Ritter is busily stacking toothpicks from a large box into what appears to be the shape of a log cabin. His focus is intense and he seems to be attempting to accomplish this balancing feat as quickly as possible.

Darren realizes he's testing the dexterity and control of his reattached limb.

"Everyone wound down enough?" Bronko asks the room.

"Just another day at the office, Chef," Cindy assures him.

Hara nods, just once.

"How's the serving arm, Ritt?" Bronko asks.

Ritter continues stacking the toothpicks. "About half an inch shorter than it was yesterday. Otherwise I appear to be all good."

Bronko nods. He looks at Darren, then back to Ritter. "So, I need you to take your crew upstate to the Henley's corporate headquarters and steal the recipe for Chicken Nuggies."

"When?" Ritter asks without hesitation or looking up from his task.

"Now."

"You're making Chicken Nuggies?" Moon asks Bronko. "I *love* Chicken Nuggies. With Big Top sauce?"

Darren looks at the faces of the rest of them.

No one seems to be concerned about the nature or implication of Chef Luck's request.

Ritter nods. "Will do, boss."

"Thanks."

Bronko turns, suppressing a grin as he briefly faces

Darren, and walks out of the Stocking & Receiving Department.

"You need something, Sparky?" Cindy asks Darren a moment later when he hasn't moved.

"Uh," he stammers.

"Reel it in," Ritter instructs Cindy.

He finally puts the toothpicks down and looks up at Darren. He lifts his arm and holds it between them.

"That was a good catch earlier, kid. Thanks."

Darren nods dumbly for approximately the twelve-thousandth time that day.

"Hey, you know," he manages, "we all work together now, right?"

They all laugh at that, even Hara.

Darren feels caught for a second, but he realizes he doesn't feel laughed at.

He's also beginning to realize why not one of these people bucked at being ordered to commit corporate espionage and theft.

PART III

INTO THE CLOWN'S MOUTH

GUIDED TOUR

Their tour guide is the apotheosis of all tour guides.

Ritter, Cindy, and Hara are dressed like tourists. Ritter and Cindy, a teenager's backpack strapped to her shoulders, both wear Henley's T-shirts while Hara is decked out in resort wear because there was no article of clothing in the gift shop that would fit him. They've mixed in with about twenty other fast-food enthusiasts (or just easily impressed road trippers) eager for a peek behind the scenes of the restaurant chain at which they've grown up polluting their bodies.

The lobby of the Henley Corporation's main corporate offices is clean, modern, opulent, and more or less exactly what you'd expect of a corporate lobby. Its only outstanding feature is a fifty-foot tableau draped from the ceiling. All the beloved characters from the Henley's mythos are painted together on it, smiling down upon all their friends who've come to visit Circus Farm.

There's Monsieur Udders, the beret-wearing cow who was created after Henley's added beef to their formerly all-chicken menu of proteins. There's Postman Potato-head, the most literally interpreted of Henley's characters with his vintage mail carrier's uniform and roasted red cranium.

They're all grouped around one of the most famous clowns in history, Redman Britches, resplendent in his silver-and-crimson costume. Britches is cradling Mrs. Henley herself, the plump and venerable chicken who was the progenitor of it all. Her eggs and chicks were the first items served when there was no Henley's, only a rickety roadside stand manned by the real Redman Britches.

Mrs. Henley wears her trademark pink-and-silver ruffled collar and colored face buttons. She doesn't smile, because none of the original artists could render a realistic chicken smiling without it looking horrifying, especially to children.

The group's tour guide, bright and bubbly with a blond perm that might've just stepped from a time machine, walks backward with perfect poise.

"Everyone is of course familiar with the animated versions of the Circus Farm family," she announces. "Whether you remember them from any of over four thousand commercials through the decades, any one of the five incarnations of the Henley's Saturday-morning cartoon, or from the related comic books, video games, and our recently launched Circus Farm education app."

"Jesus," Cindy mutters.

"You're riveted," Ritter informs her.

"Right."

"What not everyone knows is Redman Britches was in fact a real clown in the 1930s, and Missus Henley was also not only a real chicken, but his star attraction. He fashioned her a costume and trained her to dance to entertain the local children in towns throughout the American South."

As she talks, the tour guide leads them out of the main lobby and down a broad corridor that branches off through marble awnings into common areas and services for the staff, including an in-house Starbucks.

"Britches the Clown also used Missus Henley as his primary food source. Using her eggs and cooking in a small Georgia shack, almost exclusively for himself, he created the recipes that eventually led to the earliest versions of the Henley's menu items we have all enjoyed for over eighty years."

They find themselves surrounded by enormous frames filled with glossy photos of the food items that became a phenomenon and transformed a regional fast-food chain into a global biochemical conspiracy.

Cindy stares horrified into the depths of a ten-times-scale Double Cluck chicken biscuit topped with cheese, bacon, a fried egg, and too-vibrant-to-be-food hollandaise sauce. It's accompanied by Henley's "clown noses," the signature miniature red roasted potatoes the chain serves in lieu of French fries.

And, of course, there are Henley's Chicken Nuggies, blown up to the size of armchairs and ready to dive into a vat of Big Top sauce.

At least the corporate headquarters doesn't smell like a Henley's restaurant.

"Finding a need to supplement his income, Britches established the first Missus Henley's Fresh Fried Egg Stand by a rural road just outside Atlanta in March of 1939. He sold fried eggs for a nickel apiece. The very first nickel ever made by a Henley's restaurant Britches kept for good luck, and it remains a source of pride for the Henley's Corporation."

The nickel in question is suspended in a floating Lucite frame erected in the middle of the corridor.

Their tour guide motions to it grandly.

It's a fake, of course.

The corridor reaches its end. Ritter stops as the rest of the group rounds the corner ahead. Cindy and Hara do the same, letting the tourists filter around them. They wait until the last body has disappeared around the corner and then Ritter removes three small webbed pouches from his pocket.

He hands one to Cindy, then one to Hara.

"Stick these in your cheek and try not to chew," he instructs them.

Cindy pops the pouch into her mouth without hesitation. "Should we even ask?"

Hara sniffs his briefly, more out of curiosity than concern. He fingers it against the inside of his cheek.

"It's something an Oknirabata came up with back in the day when they were worried about cameras and mirrors trapping their souls."

"Okay-whatta?"

"Give it a few minutes to seep and no artificial eye can see you. Works wonders in the micro-surveillance age."

"But real people can still see us?" Cindy asks.

"For now."

They all suck on their acrid-tasting flavor pouches concocted by some Australian spirit magician before any of their grandparents were born. When Ritter gives them the nod, they make their way to a reserve elevator bank in the back of the main level, away from all the foot traffic and bustle of the lobby and commons. There are four elevators there, one with its doors open and a sign proclaiming it to be in disuse hung from a chain between them.

"Moon?" Ritter calls out.

His tiny, greasy-haired head pops out from the side of the elevator. The rest of him follows. He's wearing an electrician's coveralls and tool belt and sucking on his own Oknirabata-recipe pouch.

"Step into my office, ladies and gents," he bids them with a grin.

They all step over the chain. Once they're inside, Moon removes it and the screwdriver he's jammed under one of the elevator door panels to keep them open.

The doors close.

"All right, suit up," Ritter announces.

They strip off their tourist attire, and Moon removes his coveralls and belt. Cindy drops her backpack and unzips it, pulling out a webbed belt and clipping it around her waist. Affixed to it, among other pouches, is a tie-down rig cradling a tactical tomahawk, the bottom of which Cindy secures to her leg to keep the handle from swinging free.

"Did you rewire the elevator?" she asks Moon.

He stares up at her blankly. "No. I dunno how to do that."

"Well, then how are we making it take us to research and development? It's got to be restricted. We didn't cop any access cards or codes."

"Ritter just said hold it for you guys!" Moon insists. "I'm not a freakin' master thief. I just eat weird things. I don't know dick about bypassing wires or whatever."

"Relax," Ritter instructs them both without raising his voice.

He removes a small inkwell from Cindy's backpack and uncorks it, motioning them to move against the back wall of the elevator.

As they watch, Ritter raises his arm and swings it in the direction of the exposed wall, splashing the inkwell's contents across it. The liquid that splatters looks like blood.

Ritter reaches out and, using the tip of his thumb, draws several arcane symbols in the viscous surface of it.

"This'll guide the elevator to wherever we want it to go. It was originally cooked up for Victorian carriage drivers lost in the dark, but it should turn this box into the same kind of deal."

He waits.

So do the rest of them.

Even Cindy looks skeptical until the elevator suddenly and violently begins to rattle. They all widen their stance and brace themselves against the walls. It stops after a few seconds, and the elevator begins to lower on its own.

"Son of a bitch," she says.

"Yeah, this heist shit looks way harder in movies," Moon adds.

"You'd almost think it was magic," Ritter says with such a deadpan delivery you'd almost miss the irony.

He corks the inkwell and places it back in the pack.

Ritter takes out a tangerine-sized glass globe filled with an iridescent purple liquid.

"This is a temporary glamour," he explains. "It's only going to last fifteen minutes, but for those fifteen minutes everyone will see us as something expected. Whatever they'd expect to see that wouldn't make them deal with an unwanted reality. So we need to work fast, but we should be solid if we do."

"Where do you get all these great toys, anyway?" Moon asks him.

Ritter shrugs. "People who work in an office steal office supplies. People who work where I was before this . . . don't."

THE ALCHEMIST

There's a decrepit 1970s-era camper permanently parked behind Sin du Jour. It has three flat tires and a boot clamped on its sole inflated wheel. Its windshield is currently more unpaid parking ticket than glass. A lone bumper sticker, faded and torn, reads, "Oaxaca '79."

Tag Dorsky is seated next to the camper's open door on the steps leading inside.

Kneeling beside him is a half-lit man with messy dark hair and an unfiltered cigarette bobbing on his lower lip.

Ryland examines the sous-chef's knife wounds closely. He squints, not because his vision is impaired, but because it's still light out and focusing is giving him a splitting headache.

"You smell like a wino dipped in other winos," Dorsky idly comments.

"Dorsky, I'm aware acting like a hippopotamus's rectum is integral to your personality, but if you could stuff it for the next few minutes?"

Ryland's brogue is pure Galway, although virtually no one in America ever can or does tell the difference. He drinks constantly, fine wine when he can both afford it and summon the effort to seek it out, and bottom shelf when he's broke or already drunk and finds he's run out of the good stuff.

He drinks because he was forced to become an alchemist by his alchemist father.

He drinks because he hates alchemy.

He drinks because he has zero talent for absolutely anything else.

"To be stabbed by a woman you didn't even sleep with for several years first," Ryland says. "Shameful. Had you an ounce of male pride you'd hang yourself with your own penis."

"Why can't we ever just go to a hospital?" Dorsky complains to no one; the heavens, it seems.

"Come inside," Ryland bids him. "Hospitals are for aristocrats and football hooligans."

Dorsky reluctantly stands and turns, trudging up the steps into the camper with Ryland right behind him.

The camper's interior is a living collage of potion bottles and stones of a thousand colors and varieties. Various other arcane implements are scattered among empty wine bottles and fast-food wrappers, most of them from Taco Bell and Henley's.

"Love what you've done with the place."

"What did I just say? Now sit there."

There's a wooden plank nailed to the wall beside the door. The center of it is permanently stained red in an erratic spatter pattern. Dorsky stares quizzically at it as he sits directly across from the strange adornment in a lawn chair from the 1950s.

"Take that thing off," Ryland instructs him, motioning at his bloody, slashed smock.

Dorsky obeys, grumbling unintelligibly.

"Lift your arm."

He does, exposing the gash where Lena splayed his flesh.

Ryland reaches into a small drawer, one among several dozen fashioned into the camper on all sides, and removes a small dove.

As Dorsky watches, the Irishman pricks the dove with a miniscule pin, drawing its blood.

"Jesus, man."

"Don't worry, I anesthetized it with Thunderbird before you arrived."

Dorsky can't tell whether or not he's joking.

Ryland sifts among the wreckage of the floor and comes up with a discarded cork. Setting the bird aside, he cuts two smaller pieces from the cork with a miniature Athame. He takes the bloodied pin and twists it once into each cork sliver, staining them both with the dove's blood.

"Are you making this shit up as you go along?" Dorsky asks.

"How would that be any different from cooking?"

Ryland abruptly twists one piece of cork into the gash under Dorsky's arm, causing him to suck in air sharply.

"What the fuck?"

"Relax. You're a very large man. It's a very small piece of cork."

Ryland twists the second bit into the knife wound on Dorsky's forearm.

"Now what?" he asks.

"It's quite simple," Ryland says.

Then he picks up the dove and smashes it between his hand and the center of the wooden plank nailed to the wall.

Dorsky actually jumps in his seat.

"Fucking psycho!"

"Yes, it's a tragedy," Ryland says wearily. "It had so much to live for, so much to accomplish. How many chickens have you butchered today, by the by?"

He removes his hand and the bird drops into a trash can at the base of the wall.

Dorsky stares at him in disbelief.

Then, one after the other, the slivers of cork in his wounds pop out on their own and fall to the floor.

Dorsky examines his flesh.

The patches that were sliced apart have now healed completely.

No trace is left.

"You're kidding me," he marvels.

"Only in so much as my life is a joke. There will be no charge. I'm on retainer. Now piss off, please."

There's a knock on the open camper door.

It's Bronko.

"Busy day," Ryland says to him. "What have you gone and done to yourself?"

"Nothing," Bronko says.

He tosses something at Dorsky, who catches it.

It's a small tube filled with Ramiel's blood.

"We need a soup that tastes and looks like that," Bronko says. "You and the line are on that, in addition to the rest of the menu. Have a tasting ready for me by the end of the day."

Dorsky stares into the tube.

He looks up at Bronko.

"We're actually doing this? Trying to snow them like this? Allensworth? His people? The fucking clans?"

"Yes."

"All right. Are you still pissed at me?"

"Yes."

"All right."

"Is this going to take terribly long, gentlemen?" Ryland asks.

"You're parked in my lot, you're on my dime, Ryland," Bronko reminds him.

"Oh, my liege," the alchemist replies dryly.

"Get it done, Tag," he says to Dorsky heavily. "You had your chance."

Dorsky grins, just a little. "Yeah. She's got some moves, I guess."

"Yeah. It's a good thing I didn't let you slice her up, huh?"

Dorsky sighs. "I wasn't really gonna—"

"Yes, you were. Now get back to work."

Bronko doesn't wait for him to reply.

Dorsky leans back in his chair, folding his arms across his chest and frowning.

"I'm sorry," Ryland says. "Can we have our little pout somewhere else?"

"You got a hot date with a bottle?"

"Two bottles. Call it a threesome."

"You dog."

Dorsky tosses the capped tube in his hand, catching it with his other.

"All right," he repeats to himself, grabbing his smock and climbing out of the camper.

Ryland closes the door behind him.

He opens a high cabinet where he keeps his reserve

stash of vino.

"Maybe a foursome," he says to no one in particular.

R&D

It looks like a living sepia photograph. Time has drained the color from the expansive production floor and replaced it with equal parts dust and rust. That is all time has done, however. From the looks of the place it stopped evolving the furnishings and equipment somewhere around the late '50s. The entire floor is also dead silent and completely deserted.

Ritter ends up sticking the glamour spell back in his pocket, unused.

There's no one to see them regardless of the form they take.

They walk between the antique commercial cooking and baking equipment, the freestanding mad-scientist laboratory stations overgrown with cloudy glass tubes and beakers. Not a single inch of the entire floor has been updated with the rest of the building.

There aren't even any visible surveillance cameras keeping an eye on the place.

Cindy asks the obvious question: "This is the research and development department of the biggest fast-food chain in the whole fuckin' world?"

"I mean, they haven't really changed the menu in a while," Moon offers.

Ritter traces a fingertip over the embossed logo on a massive deli slicer.

"'American Slicing Machine Company,'" he reads. "Now that's old-school."

He looks up at them, his expression unreadable.

"Well," he says. "This doesn't make any sense at all, does it?"

"Ritt."

They all turn toward the simple utterance as if it's gunfire.

Hara never speaks unless he has something important to say.

"What's up, man?" Ritter asks.

"Some of the logos on this equipment aren't logos," he says in a voice far too light and young to accompany his Minotaur's frame.

Hara points to a freestanding bread oven shaped like an atomic-age incubator.

Ritter moves to the aging industrial womb, leaning close to examine its red, blue, and white brand stamp. Although it has the same aesthetic of the rest of the vintage logos on the floor, the language of its letters is completely anachronistic to the time period.

"Ancient Arabic?"

"Ancient North Arabian," Hara corrects him.

Moon shrugs, unimpressed. "So what? So they bought a bunch of Arab-made ovens an' shit. Who cares?"

"Like the man said." Ritter moves to the next bread oven and examines its stamp. The color pattern and logo are the same, but the letters are different. "These aren't logos."

"How do you know?"

"A lesson on industrial manufacturing and geopolitics in the 1950s aside? Because there's more than one and each word is different and it's an eighteen-hundred-year-old dead fucking language."

"Oh. Right."

Ritter leans away from the bread oven and slowly turns in place, examining the dilapidated production floor with an entirely new perspective.

"How many of them are there? How many different words?"

"A few dozen, at least," Hara says.

"So what does that mean?" Moon asks.

Ritter and Hara seem to confer silently through a quick series of brow movements.

It's unsettling to watch.

Ritter nods. "It's a summoning lock."

"You know that doesn't answer my question, right?"

"It's like a keypad lock, only it's spread out on different objects and the keys are all these inscriptions. You have to speak a certain number of them aloud in the right order and it summons whatever the lock is protecting."

"Which is what, in this case?" Cindy asks.

"And why the fuck is there a magical lock in a disused floor of Henley's corporate offices?" Moon adds.

"I don't know," Ritter says. "Everything we've seen so far has been technological and man-made."

"It doesn't matter," Hara adds. "There's no way to deduce the order of the summon."

"And generally speaking, if you try to summon what's beyond the lock and speak the words in the wrong order, very bad things happen."

"So we abort?" Cindy asks.

"Oh!" Moon exclaims suddenly, in a way that suggests a cartoon lightbulb has materialized above his head. "Oh! Oh shit!"

Cindy frowns at him. "What, for chrissakes?"

Moon is grinning. "The hack, man! Back in the lobby. When I rolled past the security station in my whole get-up. One of the rent-a-hacks. He had this ink on his arm. I thought it was, like, a tribal thing. But it was this shit." Moon points at the embossed Arabian script. "He had it all down the inside of his wrist."

Cindy looks to Ritter. "He must've written it down to remember the order."

He nods. "How many words, Moon?"

Their anointed taste tester thinks.

"Five?"

"You asking me or telling me?"

"Five," Moon says again, resolutely.

"Can you remember the order?"

"Uh, I think if I look around at these things I can pick them out."

Ritter looks up at Hara. "Can you sound out the words?"

Hara doesn't speak or nod, but he also doesn't have to in order to make himself understood.

"All right. Moon, pick out the logos."

Moon removes his smartphone from one of his pockets. "I'll snap 'em and arrange 'em in order. No worries."

He begins skittering between the half-century-old machines and examining each logo.

Cindy steps close to Ritter, speaking for his ear only.

"Even if his pan-fried brain can work this shit out, are you sure we want to go cracking this seal?"

"Only other option is to abort."

"Yeah, I know, but we have no idea if this is even protecting what we came here for. And if not, I'm not sure we want to find out why a billion-dollar corporation needs a magical lock."

"Our only other option is to abort," he repeats.

"Well, under the circumstances maybe that's the advisable option."

"If we abort," Ritter explains carefully and for her benefit, "then Bronko has no choice but to hang what Allensworth brought us upside-down, slit its throat, bleed it, and butcher it. You good with that?"

Cindy doesn't answer.

"I know we don't generally make a habit of talking feels in the basement," he continues, "and I don't particularly want to start. So I'll just come right out and say I'm not good with it. It's the difference between serving demons and being one."

"That's a pretty fine distinction," she says.

"No, it's not."

"No, it's not," Cindy echoes, however begrudgingly.

"I got it!" Moon announces. "I think I got it, anyway. It should be . . . yeah, I think I got it."

He hands off the phone to Hara, who holds it and stares above Moon's head at Ritter doubtfully.

"Are you sure, Moon?" Ritter asks. "We don't have any way to know what summoning this thing incorrectly will do to us."

"I got this," Moon assures him, then immediately amends the statement with, "I ninety-nine percent got this."

"Okay then."

Moon hands his phone to Hara.

Hara takes it and swipes the screen with his thumb five times, staring at it intently.

He looks up and nods at Ritter.

Ritter nods back.

Hara speaks five words unintelligible to Western ears.

"How long does this shit usually take?" Moon asks a few seconds later.

As if in answer, the ground beneath their feet rumbles violently and begins to split apart.

It doesn't separate from a perfect puzzle-piece seam down its center; it rends jagged concrete from jagged concrete. Ritter grabs Moon by his collar and pulls him to the side, stabilizing him easily with one hand. Hara and Cindy back up hastily.

A deep, booming laugh like the opening of some children's program from Hell rises up from the sudden crevasse.

A gargantuan bust rises from the depression. Its aspect is that of the famous clown, Redman Britches himself, yet twisted somehow. The mouth is too wide, the teeth a little too jagged.

And its eyes are utterly evil.

There's a flash of many colors in the dark hollow of

that mouth, and then they are all bombarded by what feels like hardened air.

It's waxy, hollow plastic. Ritter extends his arm and closes his hand around a sphere.

They are plastic balls.

They are plastic balls like the ones filling a million fiberglass playground pits.

A seemingly endless stream of them is flying lightning-fast from the clown's mouth, and they are beginning to pile up around Ritter's feet. In seconds they've filled the room and risen to waist-level. All of them try to wade from the path of the endless volleys, but there is no escape, no end.

Ritter tries to yell instructions and Cindy tries to answer, but their voices are shouts underwater.

At some point the ground beneath their feet disappears and all four of them are slipping through.

The entire world has become a child's playpen.

There's no bottom.

REPLACEMENT PARTS

"This is fucking amazing," Lena says around a mouthful of cupcake.

"Lemon cake, blackberry frosting," Nikki informs her. "It's one of my specialties."

They're tucked away in Nikki's pastry kitchen, which is removed from the majority of the Sin du Jour chaos and which Lena is finding she much prefers.

Bronko has Dorsky and the rest of the chefs working on the rest of the menu, as well as a substitute dish for Ramiel's blood.

He's tasked Nikki and Lena with coming up with a way to pass off fake angel wings.

It's not Nikki's usual gig, and she was reluctant to leave Ramiel with Boosha and her stray-dog sidekick, but Bronko obviously wanted to give Lena some time away from the staff after the second blood match in the courtyard, and Nikki didn't want her to be alone.

Besides, they're proving to be an effective team.

Since Ramiel's wings, and presumably all angel wings, possess no actual meat, they're experimenting with turning potatoes and fried dough into some type of crisp that looks like the plucked husk of Ramiel's feathers.

"What kind of dip should we do with these what we've got them perfected?" Nikki asks as she delicately cuts a thin slice of potato into the appropriate shape.

"I do a pretty wicked herb dip that might work."

"It needs to be hot. Like, scorching. Demons only eat shit that comes out like lava later."

Lena flashes back to the appetizers Bronko put her and Darren on when they first arrived.

"Right. Of course."

Nikki grins. There's sadness in it that Lena realizes is sympathy.

"Probably stupid to ask if you're still having a hard time with everything," Nikki says. "Being that, you know, you guys just got here."

Lena shrugs. "It is what it is. I'm trying to keep my head down and go with the flow."

"That's right. Bronko said you were a soldier."

"What's that got to do with anything?"

"That just sounded like something a soldier would say."

Lena thinks about it for a moment. "I guess so. Quick adjustments. That's what my first team leader told me."

"I know you stayed for your friend, but thank you."

"For what?"

"Staying. Not letting the rest of them vote to kill Ramiel. I couldn't live with it."

"Then how do you work here?"

Nikki puts down the knife and potato in her hands and rubs her palms against her apron.

"Well," she begins thoughtfully. "For starters, the pay is four or five times what you'll make at any restaurant in Manhattan."

Lena frowns. "That's the reason?"

Nikki giggles. "It makes a difference, and when the shock has worn off you'll agree. Trust me."

Lena nods.

She can't argue with the truth or wisdom of that.

"But no, it's not just the money. It's two main things, really. I love food. I love cooking. I love baking. And the food we get to make here, the product and techniques we have access to—"

"Like angels?"

"It's not usually like that. But it's amazing and it's like nothing else you'll find or anything else you'll get to do anywhere in the world, Lena. I swear. It's amazing. Some of the things you'll make. The things you'll taste."

Lena rolls those words over in her head for a few moments.

Then: "What's the second main thing?"

"Wonder," Nikki says, utterly earnest in her delivery

of the word.

Lena blinks in confusion. "I . . . what?"

"Wonders. You get to see and touch wonders. Things you only thought existed in fantasy and things you never even imagined. And just when you think you've seen the most wondrous thing ever, you see something even more incredible. Magical things and creatures and . . . just . . . yeah. I work here for the wonders."

"Wow," Lena says, because she can't think of anything else to say.

She stares openly at Nikki, thinking no one Lena has ever met has been so brazenly, confidently innocent about their life and career. Darren has an innocence that draws her, but much of it is born of uncertainty and fear that often frustrates her to no end.

This woman, Nikki, knows who she is and what she wants from the world around her, and she makes no apologies, indirect or otherwise.

Lena decides Nikki is the first person she's met at Sin du Jour whom she genuinely likes.

"I make a buffalo chicken dip," Lena finds herself offering suddenly. "We could kick up the heat."

Nikki is instantly excited. "That sounds so good!"

Lena grins. She begins gathering up the potato feathers they've fashioned thus far.

"Let's fry these and see what we've got."

"You look like you're finally having fun."

Lena wipes away her grin with a clearing of her throat.

"Let's not get ahead of ourselves," she says.

Nikki nods solemnly. "Of course." But her grin remains.

MRS. HENLEY

Ritter is fourteen years old, as thin and fragile as a shadow over glass, and he's hanging on to the back of a black-market Gunhound pushing forty knots up the Amazon River.

The spray feels like hot tears on his face and the shrieks of the Harpy twenty feet off their stern makes him cringe.

His father is yelling at Ritter to help him stabilize the net cannon while he lines up the shot.

They're paying a thousand reais a pound for Harpy flesh back in Macapá.

His father is yelling at Ritter to open his eyes, to stop being a pussy.

But Ritter doesn't want to look.

He doesn't want to see the creature's face, the twisted perversion of femininity in its aspect or its eyes sinking black eternal, boring into his soul and trying to tempt his body at the same time.

The awful shriek of the Harpy—

—becomes chanting.

Chanting.

Heavy and choral and inhumanly monotone.

It's somewhere far off.

Half unconscious and trapped in memory, Ritter thinks it's his alarm clock.

His eyes flutter open and he sits up.

The four of them are lying on rough, dirt-covered stone.

Ritter looks up.

They're underground.

They're in some kind of subterranean chamber. It devolves into shadow several yards away, the only visible entrance or exit. The rest appears to be solid rock.

"Fuck me," Moon moans as he also sits up.

"Was there tequila?" Cindy asks groggily.

Ritter looks down at Hara.

He's awake, eyes open, reclining passively and staring at the stalactites rimming the ceiling.

"Everybody's okay," Ritter says aloud, although it's clear he's informing himself, not them.

Moon snorts. "Loose definition."

"The summoning spell must've transmutated through some kind of portal," Ritter tells them.

"So where are we?" Cindy asks.

He shrugs. "We could be underneath the Henley's building. We could be a thousand miles away. I have no idea."

"No reception," Moon announces, iPhone in hand.

"Not a single fucking dot."

"Not surprising."

"This was supposed to be a straight job," he whines. "The human world for a change. Daylight. Steel and concrete. A building with a conscientious janitorial staff."

"Tell it to the air force," Cindy instructs him, her sarcasm unmasked.

"Everybody on their feet," Ritter orders them.

The foursome stand, and after a moment of reclaiming their bodies and bearings, the chanting moves to the forefront of their attention.

"That's never good."

"No," Ritter says, "but it's a start."

He leads and they all follow the unintelligible chanting through the shadows and to the top of an outcropping.

Ritter motions at them to stay low, stay concealed behind the rocks.

He's the first to take it all in, but the rest are soon shoulder-to-shoulder with him.

The cavern below is vast, lit by torches each the size of a small bonfire.

The source of the chanting is clowns.

Hundreds of clowns.

They're all dressed and painted similarly to Henley's founder and other chief mascot. However, these are ghoulish, nightmare doppelgängers. Their costumes are all in dirty, aging tatters. Their painted faces are disfigured, leprous. The paint itself is browning, yellowing, and falling away with the strips of flesh it was long ago sloshed upon. What's visible beneath the holes in their clown suits is more mush than skin.

They're all rotting, inside and out.

It's nothing Ritter and his crew haven't seen before, even if it is decorated differently.

The clowns are reanimated corpses.

They're arranged in rows of ten and twenty, genuflecting and chanting in unison, all of them facing the far end of the cavern.

There, set upon a gargantuan pedestal painted like an old-time jack-in-the-box, is a nest. The nest is composed of enough wicker strands to populate a Pier One Imports franchise.

Perched inside the nest is Mrs. Henley.

There's no mistaking her. She's made up exactly as she is in all the historical photos and vibrant cartoon advertising throughout the decades.

She is, however, at least a hundred times the size of a normal chicken.

When she clucks, and she frequently does, it sounds like the funeral horn of some Viking god.

"Everyone else sees a legion of undead clowns worshipping a giant chicken, right?" Moon asks.

"Yes."

"Yeah."

Hara nods.

Moon is visibly relieved. "Okay, good."

An ancient conveyer belt is tilted up to meet Mrs. Henley's manhole cover–sized cloaca. From that gargantuan opening through which a normal chicken would lay its eggs, raw Chicken Nuggies are constantly falling a dozen at a time. They're already formed into their signature circus-themed shapes of breadcrumb hats and oversized floppy shoes.

The raw Nuggies roll down the conveyor belt, where a line of necrotic clowns douses them with batter. The other end of the conveyor belt is angled above the largest commercial fryer ever conceived by man or demon. Another battalion of clowns is charged with raising the fryer rack cage on a chain-link pulley and dumping the cooked Nuggies into a series of fifty-gallon plastic tubs with wheels.

The tubs are piled to the brim and beyond and then pushed by clowns across the cavern to a large opening in the rock draped with industrial plastic curtains. Each one disappears through those murky hanging strips, no doubt to be frozen before being dispatched by the truck-, plane-, and trainload to Henley's restaurants across the world.

Ritter and the rest of them watch the entire process unfold, each of their minds processing the ramifications of what they're witnessing.

"I never thought I'd say this," Moon groans, "but I think I'm going to be sick. I practically lived on that shit those two semesters of college I did."

"Eggs come out of a chicken's ass too," Cindy points out.

"Not the same thing!" Moon insists. "Not *nearly* the same thing!"

"Shut up, Moon," Ritter hisses.

Cindy can almost see his wheels spinning as he tries to formulate a way around this sudden, grotesque revelation and reach their goal.

"We're aborting now, right?" she asks him, and it's clear the question is rhetorical.

Ritter doesn't answer her.

"Ritt, it's over. There's no recipe to steal. We're not taking that fucking thing with us. Look, we came here to do some simple corporate espionage. Maybe have to escape a man-made cage at worst. But this place is enchanted up the ass, as dark as it gets, and if they catch us here, we will stay here. Do you feel me?"

"I gotta agree with her, man," Moon adds.

Ritter looks from Cindy to him, then at Hara.

The big man only shrugs.

"Fine, we abort," Ritter says. "How the hell do we even get out of here, though? There's no return access the way we came."

Cindy motions with a flick of her head down into the cavern. "We go out with the Nuggies."

"Through the army of zombie clowns?" Moon asks.

"They're obviously animated to perform specific tasks. That's why they're down here. They probably won't even notice us as long as we don't fuck with the chicken or them harvesting and transporting those god-awful things it's shitting."

"Please don't say that," Moon practically begs.

Ritter is looking down over the subterranean valley of Henley's minions, considering Cindy's logic.

"All right," he says a moment later. "Let's try it."

Ritter leads them down slowly and cautiously through the rocky outcropping to the main level of the cavern.

They stay low and tight, moving across the darkly enchanted production floor as quickly and stealthily as possible.

The clowns notice them immediately.

They attack the four of them almost as immediately.

"Fucking genius!" Moon shouts at Cindy.

"Educated guess," she mutters, unhooking the tomahawk from where it's strapped to her thigh.

The back three rows of worshippers are lumbering at them in rotting waves. They all bare pointed, dwindling, yellowed teeth and their throats emit the most guttural and disturbing outraged cry imaginable.

"All right, then," Ritter says calmly.

Hara nods at him and bolts forward with shocking speed for a man of his bulk. Both of his arms are stretched out to the sides as he literally falls on the attacking wave and takes four of them down with the blunt use of simple physics.

Cindy swings her tomahawk into the melted face paint of the first clown who closes range. A second one loses its mandible to a swipe of the tomahawk's blade, and a third has his nose split down the center.

Ritter has a variety of magical last resorts concealed on his person, but he refuses to view their current situation as a last resort. Instead he relies on fourteen years of hapkido training and legs like battering rams to knock down and force back the oncoming undead. Those that lumber too close to kick have their joints clamped down on and are thrown like the sacks of soiled refuse their smell so closely resembles.

Moon fades into the background, but in his own head he's the spell-caster he always played during teenage games of Dungeons & Dragons, launching magical assaults from behind the action.

Unfortunately, he never had the ambition, aptitude, or attention span to become a real wizard.

Still, they manage to lay waste to the first two waves with no casualties or serious injury.

But the rest of the clowns are thick behind their fallen fellows and pressing forward.

There's no way for one of them to make it past the clowns to the plastic curtained entrance, let alone the whole team.

Glancing behind and to the side of their position frantically, Ritter spots a smaller, uncovered tunnel hollowed into the rock less than fifty yards away.

There's no one between them and its shadowy mouth.

"There!" he yells at the others. "Break left! Stay behind me!"

He doesn't wait for them to obey before charging toward the tunnel, trusting in the time they've worked together and their faith in him.

Moon is the first behind him. Cindy has to grab Hara by his mountain range shoulders and pry him off the three concaving husks he's currently clubbing with his arms. Hara relents easily, following her as they both run after Moon and Ritter.

There are no turns or openings down the length of

the tunnel, only a narrow straightaway. They have no choice but to press forward, following the winding path wherever it leads.

"They're behind us!" Cindy informs Ritter on the run.

"I kind of figured," he calls back.

The tunnel dead-ends at a large wooden door.

A locked door.

It's sealed with a rusted wrought-iron padlock the size of a cannonball.

"Open it," Ritter instructs Cindy breathlessly.

"You really want to find out what they keep locked up down here?"

Past the shadows through which they've come, they can hear the hollow footfalls of oversized shoes on stone.

"Just fucking do it! We don't have another choice!"

Cursing almost a complete history of male pejoratives, Cindy hefts her tomahawk and bashes open the ancient padlock with four swings.

Ritter pushes past her, through the door, and ushers them quickly inside.

"Hara, get on this!" he orders after closing the door behind them.

Hara heaves his near-four-hundred-pound bulk against the door's interior and leaves it there.

He's better than any lock, any barricade, any chair under a knob.

REDMAN BRITCHES

They've arrived in the middle of the second act of a grand puppet show.

Later they'll talk about what each of them expected to find behind the locked door in that moment of madness. Yet as Hara braced the door against the methodical thumping of bodies on the other side, Ritter and Cindy sealing its seams with their hands, none of them expected to look over their shoulders and see dancing marionettes.

The whole room looks like a dirt-floor tent show from the turn of the century. There's a makeshift stage upon which large circus props wait under a layer of dust, red velvet curtains drawn back and bound with faded golden twine. A battered hundred-year-old trunk sits in the center of the room beside a lone chair. The chair is facing the miniature puppet theater standing against the rock wall.

On its mock stage, tethered figures of knights and horses and dragons are engaged in an epic battle. The steeds whinny and the swords clash and the knights exclaim, all of these sound effects created by the same skilled voice expertly thrown from stage right to stage left.

"I'm tripping balls, man!" Moon insists. "Gotta be!"

"I see it too," Ritter calmly reassures him as he continues to clamp on the doorjamb with his bare hands.

The sound of sword clangs and horse cries and dragon's breath dies out.

The motion of the puppets ceases, reducing them to lifeless things dangling from string.

Another clown emerges from behind the puppet theater, smiling an oversized smile with his perfectly painted mouth.

"Shit," Cindy hisses, raising her gore-slicked tomahawk and preparing to rush forward.

Ritter reaches out and grabs hold of her wrist, restraining her.

"Hold it," he says calmly.

The rest of the clown is clean and freshly painted, as well. Likewise, his Redman Britches costume, although somewhat faded with age, is free of tears and well maintained.

"You can turn loose of the door, young people," he assures them in a warm, very human voice.

As he says that they all realize the clamoring on the other side of the door has ceased.

"That troop of hellions is vicious, but they also aren't

much on attention. If they can't see it right in front of them they lose focus fairly quickly. They're halfway back to placating Missus Henley with all that chanting mess. Helps her make the Nuggies, you know."

"You're him, aren't you?" Ritter asks the clown. "Britches. The real one."

Redman Britches nods. "What're you folks doing down here? Who are you?"

"Thieves," Ritter answers simply.

"What are you here to steal?"

"The recipe for your Chicken Nuggies."

Britches stares at him. Perhaps he's searching for the root of some joke. Finding none, he casts his glance over the rest of them.

Then he bursts out laughing.

"Well, then, I guess you four surely happened upon the surprise of your lives."

Ritter releases his grip on the door.

The others tentatively follow his lead, stepping away from the heavy slab of oak.

"To say the least," Moon confirms.

Ritter looks back at the door, then at the clown.

"You didn't make those things, did you? Or that chicken? You're a prisoner here."

Britches stops laughing.

He nods solemnly. "Most of them wanted to be me

once. We trained them to go out to our stands all across the country and entertain the children, as I did. That they ended up down here is a service none of them wanted. As for my prison, I created it myself long ago. He just put a lock on the door."

"He?" Cindy asks.

Britches smiles once again beneath his clown makeup.

Despite that, or because of it, he suddenly looks like the sad clown.

"I never thought I'd get to tell this story to anyone. Thieves or not, I surely am glad you're here to listen. I only hope one of you lives to remember the tale. I doubt it, but I hope. I purely do."

Britches looks behind him, then around at the rest of the room, frowning.

"We seem to be suffering from a lack of seating."

"We're fine like we are," Cindy tells him. "Get on with it."

The clown bows grandly. "Your wish is my command, madam."

Britches turns and leaps up onto his small stage. Reaching into a prop box, he withdraws a flat, dark circle and with a flourish turns it into a stovepipe hat two feet high. Doffing it to his audience gratefully, Redman Britches pops the hat onto his dark crimson wig and begins his tale with bardlike projection and enunciation.

"I learned the clowning trade from my daddy, you see. He was with Master Styrgess and the Traveling Brocade for fifteen years before the typhoid took him. Then it was my turn. But I came along at a bad time for carnies. The crowds and the money were thinning with every town where our tent was raised and struck. Styrgess fired me after only three years.

"He gave me that there trunk full of half-broken props as severance, laughing when he did. And that was all I had, a weather-beaten trunk. And Missus Henley, of course. I trained her myself from a chick, hoping she'd help bring in a bigger crowd. She was nimble in her day. She preferred jazz, but that was a little . . . racy for the young ones. Oh, and the children adored her. After my untimely dischargement I would've starved if not for her, in more ways than one."

By now Moon has taken it upon himself to occupy the room's sole chair. He reaches into his pocket and removes a half-rolled-up bag of M&M's. He unfurls it and pops several into his mouth as he looks up at the stage.

Cindy stares at him as if she's watching a primate in a National Geographic special.

Ritter is listening to Britches intently.

Hara is as well, but he won't move off the door.

"I set up my little roadside stand. Times improved. I

even rented a little shack. I opened my first indoor restaurant. I decided to get rid of all this damned junk in the trunk, put it to better use. I don't even know why I bothered, but I scoured through this old trunk, looking for anything I might want to keep before I sold it to the junker man. I found it at the very bottom, just as peaceful and unassuming as you might please."

"Found what?" Moon asks, peering over his shoulder into the trunk beside the chair.

"Why, the lamp, of course!" Britches announces with a theatrical sweep of his arm.

Moon, Cindy, and Hara all trade confused looks.

"A genie," Ritter deduces with no satisfaction. "A fucking genie."

"What? Like Aladdin?"

"More like Grimm's Aladdin," Ritter says. "They're the oldest and most fucked-up con men on Earth."

"It must've been stuck down there for ages," Britches continues, lost in the memory and his performance now. "Just waiting. Waiting. I took a rag to it just to polish it up, thinking it might be worth more than scrap. What it turned loose when I rubbed it with that rag and how it grabbed hold of me was something bigger and more thrilling than any ring in any circus."

"What did you wish?" Ritter asks with uncustomary impatience.

The question seems to finally break through the revel of the stage. Britches looks directly at him, more the man beneath the makeup when he answers, "I wished to be able to make enough of my Nuggies to feed the world."

"And he did that out there to your chicken."

Britches nods, suddenly fighting back tears.

"You had to figure after that he wasn't exactly kosher," Cindy says carefully.

"Of course I did! My next wish was for him to undo what I'd done. He used that one to take over my business. Instead of unmaking my wish, he undid my part in it. After that he used his infernal magic to . . . to . . ."

Cindy finishes the thought: "Sell chicken biscuits to two-thirds of the whole fucking world."

"To gain wealth, power, and to pollute the bodies and souls of men. It all feeds him. He used to come down here to taunt me. He grew tired of that decades ago."

"You don't look that old," Moon points out.

"My connection to him keeps me as I was."

"That's only two wishes," Ritter says. "What did you do with the third?"

"I never made the third. By then I'd seen what he was. I knew he'd only twist it and do something even more horrible, to me or to the world or both. He's evil, and he's smarter than me, smarter than a man."

Moon peers over the edge of the trunk. "Is the lamp

still in here?"

"Of course not," Britches the Clown says.

Ritter sighs. "Probably ten thousand miles from here behind fifty yards of titanium surrounded by Blackwater motherfuckers."

"Oh, no," Britches corrects him. "He keeps it close. He just keeps it where no soul can possibly get at it."

"Where?"

The clown looks past them, at the door.

And past that, too.

They all follow his gaze.

Ritter is the first one to put it together.

"Fuck me," he breathes.

Cindy looks back at him. "What?"

"It's under the goddamn hen, isn't it? In the nest?"

Britches nods.

"You've gotta be kidding me."

"Makes sense," Ritter says. "In context."

"Right."

"Do you need the lamp to make your final wish?" Cindy asks the clown.

"No. Once you rub it you're connected to that foul thing. You can summon him at will. Command him. It all seems so godly at first."

"So just wish for that chicken to move so we can get to the goddamn lamp and make the fucker let us out of here," Cindy says impatiently.

Ritter is already shaking his head. "Genie One-Oh-One. We'd be doing the same thing Bozo here is talking about."

"Britches," the clown corrects him, haughtily.

"Right. We wish for the genie to move the chicken, he knows why we want him to do it, so he moves it on top of us or moves the whole fucking nest to Brazil or whatever."

Moon finishes that train of thought: "And we're trapped down here with no moves left watching puppets fuck until we die."

"My puppet shows are for all ages. And watch your language, young man."

"Fuck you, clown."

"Point is," Ritter says firmly, "it's not hard to kill a genie. Especially with the benefit of having read *One Thousand and One Nights*."

He looks at Cindy pointedly.

She nods. "Right."

"Wait. What?" Moon asks.

"Never mind," Cindy snaps at him. "What he's saying is the genie can't see it coming. He can't have time to adapt. He's had Britches here clocked for the better part of a century. We need to put someone new on the lamp, throw him off. Give us time to hit him with the unexpected."

Ritter walks away from them all, lost in thought.

"What we do about that, Ritt?" Cindy asks, trying very hard and failing not to sound helpless.

"We get you the lamp," he says.

"How?"

"And why her?" Moon asks.

Ritter is eyeing the prop box on Britches's stage.

There's a chicken carved into one of the square's panels.

"Your chicken," he says to the clown. "How did she make the eggs?"

"Excuse me?"

"Your fried egg stand. You said all you had was that trunk and the chicken. The trunk didn't impregnate her."

"I camped near a farm. Missus Henley wandered at night."

"And found a rooster."

"I suppose."

Ritter turns and looks back at Cindy.

For the first time all day he cracks a grin.

COCK OF THE WALK

The clowns are gone.

They're not gone, of course, but they're not waiting outside the door to Britches's theater cell.

Ritter creeps to the mouth of the tunnel, being careful to stay behind the veil of shadows. Cindy follows close behind.

"Stay close to the rocks, behind the torchlight, and take your time working around toward the nest."

She nods.

The two of them break from the mouth of the tunnel in opposite directions, tracing the rocky curve of the cavern walls encircling Henley's grotesque production floor. The undead Britches clones don't pick up on their presence this time.

Halfway to the nest, Ritter pulls out a two-way and whispers into it. "Moon, have him make the wish. And don't fuck up the wording."

A deafening, horrible crowing splits the cloistered air of the cavern.

It sounds like a thousand roosters cursing the sunrise

rather than greeting it.

Mrs. Henley's undead harlequins cease their chanting.

Dozens of overripe heads turn.

Their cataract-covered eyes fall on the source of the crowing.

It's not a thousand roosters.

It's one rooster.

The cock stands a full story taller than Mrs. Henley herself and is even wider in body. He rises up on tree trunk legs across the cavern from the nest in front of the tunnel leading to Britches's cell.

The rooster spreads his burnt-sienna wings and crows again.

He's calling for a mate.

Ritter leans out of the shadows and motions to the other side of the cavern for Cindy to double-time it to the nest.

Mrs. Henley raises wings that belong on a Gulfstream jet. They struggle against the suction they create before she finally rips them free of her own body. The G-force actually sends spearlike bristles splintering from her perch. When she begins flapping them, however, the motion creates an invisible wave so powerful it bowls over a dozen clowns nearest their holy dais.

It takes almost a full minute and another air-threshed

row of undead clown flesh before Mrs. Henley builds enough momentum to lift her enormous bulk out of the nest. It tears the lip off the front, raining down more bristles, and when she touches down past the dais it shakes the entire cavern and crushes a nap circle of prone bodies.

The rest of the worshipping masses begin to cautiously surround the uber-hen, trying hopelessly to corral and pacify her. Even the clowns manning the conveyor belt, the fryer, and the plastic wheelbarrows abandon their posts, drawn inextricably to this massive disruption in their darkly enchanted routine.

Cindy braces herself against the rough-hewn rock, waiting.

It's like watching children trying to stop two planets from colliding with their bare hands. Mrs. Henley tramples a field of her own minions as she squawks and flaps and bounds toward the rooster. Torches are ripped down, spreading fire across the dirt and rocks.

Cindy breaks from the wall, dashing through the decimated remains of what now resemble pulverized clown corpses. The ones who weren't trampled, or were only knocked aside and dazed, turn their attention to her.

When Mrs. Henley and the rooster conjured by Britches's final wish collide, it shakes the cavern like an epic tectonic shift.

Cindy takes the heads off three of the clowns between her and the nest with her tomahawk before casting it off. She leaps up past the dais and grabs two handfuls of nest. Her arms are ready to hoist her the rest of the way up when a lethal weight suddenly vise-grips her legs and anchors her down. Cindy only clenches her fists tighter around the thick sprigs, drawing blood.

She spares a glance over her strained shoulder to see three clowns grasping her legs.

And more are coming.

They're not as fast as Ritter, however. He heads off the oncoming hordes, launching a leaping front kick into the back of the center clown holding on to Cindy's leg and practically puts his shriveled heart through his chest. He pulls a second off her with brute force while keeping the rest at bay with his legs.

"Get it done!" Ritter calls up to her.

Cindy kicks the last clown's gloved hands away and pulls herself up and over the crushed lip of the nest.

The smell that immediately assaults her nostrils very nearly causes her to vomit, the result of which would probably be indistinguishable from the sludge in which she lands at the bottom of the nest.

Cindy puts a mental clamp on the churning in her gut, holds her nose, and plunges in elbow-deep.

"Any fucking time, Cin!" Ritter calls from outside the

nest.

Her right hand finally closes around something smooth and metallic and round.

She grips it and yanks it free of the muck.

It looks exactly like you would expect a genie's lamp to look, albeit caked in offal.

"Is that what you came for, little dove?" the genie himself asks her.

Cindy turns and looks up.

He's hovering several feet above the conveyer belt, arms folded magnanimously over the lapels of his designer suit and a five-hundred-dollar cornflower tie. His legs dangle loosely, but gracefully, and rather than patent-leather loafers filled with the reflection of firelight he's wearing a pair of curled-toe Mojari shoes embellished with green and blue beads.

"Come to me," the genie bids her.

Cindy climbs up the side of the nest, lamp in hand, to stand perched just beyond the top of the conveyor belt.

The genie looks down on her benevolently.

His smile is radiant, angel-like.

Or it would be if Cindy hadn't recently laid eyes on a true angel.

She knows better now.

"You have but to rub the lamp. Rub it and you will command every drop of magic in the cup of my being.

You will be in the position of a god."

Cindy frowns. "In your thrall, you mean."

He laughs. "You give me far too much credit, little dove. I am but a humble servant. I remain only what the clown's greed has made me. I thrill to free of it, and all of this madness. I beg of you, allow me to serve a nobler mistress in you."

She nods. "I bet that shit worked like Spanish fly before the Internet, too."

The genie doesn't appear to get it.

Cindy presses her palm flat against the filthy body of the lamp and caresses it deeply.

She immediately feels the connection, like an invisible tether gently drawing her to the genie and vice versa.

"Yes," he breathes.

"I wish," she begins.

"Yes?" he asks her, hungrily.

"I wish for you to be mortal."

His smile disappears.

His body drops with a total lack of grace and coordination down onto the conveyor belt.

It's that simple.

There's no divine flashing of lights, no thundering sound effects.

He's just a guy trying to stay upright on a treadmill.

"You clever harlot!" he swears up at her, his eyes on

the moving tract beneath him as he stumbles, recovers, and stumbles again.

"Do you have a name?" she calmly asks the spirit-made-flesh. "A real name?"

"Why?" he asks back, distracted by the task of keeping up with the motion of the conveyor belt. "What is my name to you?"

Her next words tip the scale from calm to bitter cold: "I made a promise to myself, years back. I promised myself I'd never again kill someone without knowing their name."

The former genie looks up from the moving conveyor belt then, his expression suddenly drawn and pale.

Then, despite his predicament, he grins.

"You'll just have to wonder, little dove."

Cindy nods.

She swings the lamp into his jaw with a yell that also splits his eardrums.

The ex-demon jilts back and lands hard atop the center of the conveyor belt, unconscious.

Ritter ascends the dais and nest beside her just in time to watch the CEO of the Henley's Corporation drift down that gently drawn slant. At the same time the painted torso of a legless clown drags itself over the side of the conveyor belt and begins slopping batter onto its former master's body, still carrying out its magically automated task.

"This seems harsh," Ritter comments without enthusiasm. "Even for him."

Cindy shrugs. "You pull him off the belt."

Ritter is silent for a moment.

Then: "Fuck it. I'm too tired."

Slathered from head to toe, the formerly enchanted CEO continues his journey to the gargantuan fryer.

When his chicken-battered form hits the boiling oil, the genie shrieks inhumanly.

And then he doesn't make a sound.

Neither Ritter nor Cindy looks away.

They've both seen worse.

In the human world completely bereft of magic, they've both seen worse.

More rag doll–torn clowns slouch toward the fryer, still rapt by the genie's lingering spell. They hoist the rack free of the cloudy brown bubbling oil. When it drains, what's left is the vague golden form of a man, as if a sculptor has keeled over just after defining his creation's most basic shape.

They tilt the heavy wire cage between its chained joints and dump the fried form into a wheelbarrow.

"Odds they actually end up serving him in some backwater Henley's?" Cindy asks as the world's largest Chicken Nuggie is wheeled through those heavy plastic curtains.

"Even money," Ritter says.

She looks down at the lamp still clutched in her bleeding, muck-covered hand, then up at Ritter.

They're too tired to laugh, but their eyes do what they can on their own.

Cindy tosses the lamp back into the swampy crater at the bottom of the nest.

The two of them stand in the cavern of burning rocks and stare out across a field of undead corpses finally laid to rest at two giant farm animals in heat frantically grinding biological vents.

"I kinda thought making that fucker mortal would reverse all of this," Cindy says. "Make it disappear or whatever."

Ritter just shakes his head.

"Life is never that clean," he assures her. "Neither is magic."

HAPPY MEALS

The five of them emerge from an industrial drainage pipe half a mile from the Henley's building.

Britches kneels in the murky pond water and cups his hands around it, splashing his face.

He vigorously rubs away his clown makeup.

"What're you going to do now?" Ritter asks him.

He breathes deeply. The face underneath, red and raw and wet as it is now, is utterly unremarkable.

"Never eat chicken again," is all he says.

Britches removes one comically large shoe, then the other.

From that second shoe he removes a small yellow-brown fold of paper.

He hands it to Ritter, who takes it curiously and unfolds it.

Scrawled on the unfolded sheet is a recipe.

Moon peers over Ritter's shoulder at the contents of the page. "Holy shit!"

"That's what you came for. I think you've more than earned it."

Ritter looks up at the man behind Redman Britches the Clown.

"But the chicken—"

"Missus Henley was magicked to produce my Nuggies, just the way I made them before I ever touched that damned lamp. She didn't change them. I promise."

Ritter nods, carefully tucking the refolded piece of paper in his pocket.

"You got a name that doesn't end in 'the Clown'?" he asks.

Britches ponders that.

"I did once. But I think I'll pick a new one."

"Okay, then."

Britches the ex-clown turns and trudges through the pond and up onto the grass, walking into the woods.

"We going back for the rental car?" Cindy asks.

Ritter shakes his head. "I feel like walking."

"I'm hungry," Moon says.

It's one of the rare occasions upon which Ritter allows Cindy to smack him upside his head.

PART IV

A BANQUET FOR DEMONS

THE MISSING INGREDIENT

The original recipe is surprisingly, even shockingly, simple: onion powder, garlic powder, black pepper, and a touch of molasses are the only real flavorings added.

And just a touch of sorghum.

It's not a chemical or a preservative, as Bronko thought.

It was the 1930s and for some reason the damn clown added some sorghum, probably from a nearby field.

They don't even have to go shopping for more ingredients. Everything they need is in the Sin du Jour pantry.

The secret is in the proportions, the exactitude of each ingredient and its ratio to each nugget. A little too much or not enough and the flavor becomes a reasonable, obvious imitation of the real thing.

They all marvel over the fact that it's only a pinch of onion powder separating mediocrity from worldwide renown and endless riches.

Well, it's that *and* an ancient, malevolent genie with dreams of making the Fortune 500 list.

Ritter, Cindy, Hara, and Moon obviously have a

doozy of a story to tell; they usually do after a run, but the newbies can see the foursome is in an uncustomary bad way when they hand the recipe over upon their return.

Bronko sent Lena and Darren out to purchase just south of a hundred pounds of venison ahead of the team's return. The consistency of the meat is perfect, but its natural flavor is far gamier than Ramiel's flesh. They have to go to great lengths to siphon that natural flavor out and reduce the meat to a blank canvas.

Bronko himself slices the venison and pounds it out into a perfectly flat and tantalizingly thin paillard.

He seasons the meat by hand according to the hand-scrawled recipe of a clown.

He grills it slowly and delicately in the thinnest covering of virgin olive oil.

He cuts them all a bite when it's ready.

They eat in silence.

No one wants to be the one to say it.

"It's off," Lena pronounces.

Bronko nods gravely. "Just enough to matter. If you know what angel is supposed to taste like."

Lena slams down her fork. "Fuck!"

"I don't even want to tell Ritter, after whatever they went through to get this recipe."

"Flour," Darren blurts out.

They look to him, immediately taken aback.

"Nuggies are battered and fried, right? Add flour to the seasoning. It's probably missing the . . . y'know . . . like, starchy, wheaty notes."

Everyone is staring at him without speaking.

Darren shifts his weight from heel to heel.

"I mean . . ." He hesitates. "Right?"

Bronko looks at Lena. "Kid's a savant."

She grins, her own gaze remaining on Darren. "Yeah. I know how to pick 'em, Chef."

It takes another dozen paillards and as many experimental measurements of flour mixed with spices and herbs, but by the end of the day everyone in the kitchen agrees they've replicated the flavor of Henley's Nuggies precisely.

And both Bronko and Lena concur it's the closest thing to angel flesh they're likely to come up with before the banquet.

"It'll have to do," he says. "We're committed now. You done good, kids. Especially for your second day."

Bronko leaves them to prep the rest of their substitute angel and wrap it until morning.

He returns a few minutes later, holding two pure-white smocks in front of him.

Each has the company's absurd cartoon chocolate cake logo imprinted on the breast.

"For the gig," he explains. "You've already earned

'em."

Darren accepts his gratefully, smiling, soaking in the acceptance.

Lena is more hesitant and reserved, but she does take the smock and briefly holds it against her torso, sizing it.

"Thanks, Chef," Darren says.

Lena only nods.

"Thank you, kids."

Bronko leaves them for real.

He has every intention of returning to his office and drinking until he passes out head down on his desk.

He makes it about halfway up the hall before his legs stop moving on their own.

Bronko has to lean back against the wall, then finds himself sliding down it until he's sitting.

The weight of it all has hit him full force, what they're attempting, what the consequences could be, and also the trajectory his life has taken since he accepted the position as executive chef of Sin du Jour.

Bronko shakes, and keeps shaking until he forces a steely calm over himself.

When he looks up Dorsky is standing above him, holding two icy bottles of some obscure IPA by their glass necks.

He hands one to Bronko, expressionless.

Bronko takes it with a steady hand.

They tap bottlenecks.

They drink.

"Is there any possible chance we get away with this, boss?"

More than the beer, his question seems to refortify Bronko, who forces his legs to carry him back up the wall until he's standing anew.

Sin du Jour's executive chef downs the rest of his beer and hands the bottle back to Dorsky.

"You should've worked harder on your knife fighting," he tells his second-in-command.

"Yeah, well." Dorsky finishes his own beer, swallowing the last bitter hard.

Bronko makes it back to his office.

He locks the door behind him.

He drinks as planned, but he never passes out over his desk.

In fact, he's awake most of the night.

A MORTAL OCCUPATION

Demons aside, the whole affair is shockingly standard, even dull, until the new busboy reaches for a dish before its Vig'nerash diner is finished and the demon splatters him all over the wall.

The venue, either surprisingly or predictably, is concealed within a Masonic lodge downtown. Lena was placed in charge of piloting one of three large cargo vans bearing the Sin du Jour logo. They're directed by one of Allensworth's men into an alley behind the turn-of-the-century building, where a stairway leads below the subbasement.

Torches light the subterranean space until Jett's crew arrives and she demands they all be replaced with the festive lighting setup she's designed for the event.

Her "crew," as it turns out, are zombies.

No one calls them that, and when Darren practically shrieks the word like a frightened child Jett almost viciously rebukes him.

"I will simply not endure that sort of animatist pejorative language," she snaps at him. "And believe me, you don't want to be brought before this company's HR department. I'm not even sure it's in this dimension."

"I'm . . . sorry?" is what Darren manages.

But they are, without dispute, the reanimated corpses of the dead.

"Most of them are from Hollywood," she explains when Lena asks the question Darren can't seem to formulate. "Sound and lighting engineers, grips, like that. You wouldn't believe how many on-set fatalities go unreported by movie studios. I take the victims off their hands and repurpose them for our events. It works out for everybody."

There are enough bubbles in that last sentence to explode a champagne bottle.

They also learn that what they mistook for a growth on Jett's ear when they met her is actually some kind of organic Bluetooth device that lets her command her undead staff as they go about lighting the banquet hall in pale reds and blues and yellows.

The rest of the venue is plain enough to make them forget they're preparing a feast for hellions. There's a main stage, empty (apparently live music is not a feature of demon gatherings). There are several dozen long feasting tables surrounded by wooden chairs arranged in two rows across the banquet hall floor. There are two special tables draped in bloodred cloth set on raised daises, one for the leaders of both the Oexial and Vig'nerash clans, and one for Allensworth and his human compatriots, all attired more or less like him.

Sin du Jour was led through a tall archway into an antechamber they were instructed to use as their staging area for the event. Lena, Darren, and the rest of the crew were hours setting up the buffet tables with their fire-lit chafing dishes and ornate food stations, as well as prepping for the individual service, when the time came to serve their very real, absolutely authentic, not-at-all-mock angel.

"It helps if you pretend they're all in costumes," Bronko advises the newbies before the guests begin to arrive. "At least at first."

But Lena and Darren are surprisingly underwhelmed when the clans began filing in for the banquet.

Physically the demons are a more severe version of Boosha: greener in skin tone, eyes and other features set farther back and spaced farther apart on their hairless heads. The protrusions of their joints are sharper and more pronounced, and they have subtle claws.

Horror movies have shown them much worse.

Lena and Darren are both more interested in the difference between the two clans.

The Oexial, being the older and more venerable contingent, are very much how you'd expect a demon to dress and act, especially if you were a regular viewer of *Buffy the Vampire Slayer* (and Darren remains a fanatic). Their elders wear arcane robes tied with braided cord, while their soldiers, the bulk of their party, are clad in frightening-looking armor fashioned from bone and volcanic rock and carved with terrifying visages and occult symbols.

The Vig'nerash, on the other hand, appear to be nouveau demons. Their higher-ups are decked out in genuine and modern Armani suits and Christian Siriano gowns. Their soldiers look more like mafia hitmen than warriors from Hell.

The difference between generations and worldviews is palpable, to say the least.

But whatever their cultural or ideological differences, they all fall on the food with equal ferocity.

The curry skulls Lena and Darren helped prep with the other apps are drained and crushed underfoot on the stone floor in minutes, it seems. The "brimstone" mole negro is licked clean from the oxtail taquitos, most of which are discarded (much to Bronko's irritation and Dorsky's silent amusement).

Allensworth even stops by the staging area to compliment on the fare designed for humans.

"You have no idea the horror stories I heard from my predecessors about the food at these things before we had an in-house caterer," Lena overhears him telling Bronko.

And then it's time for the main courses.

"Put it out of your heads," Bronko has instructed them all. "Just slam it out like any other menu and put what it is and what they think it is and what we don't want them to think it's not all out of your heads."

So they do.

Lena and Darren help plate the crisps they've fashioned to emulate plucked angel feathers, along with the intense buffalo dipping sauce to accompany them.

Pacific, Mr. Mirabel, and the high-strung new server/busboy who insists on everyone calling him "Raw Dog" pick up the plates and carry them from the staging area.

As they all begin ladling the ghost pepper gazpacho they're passing off as angel blood soup into bowls, every one of the chefs tries not to think about what just a single demon questioning a single dish might mean to their collective future.

The soup has been served and they begin prepping the angel paillard entrées when Bronko appears beside Dorsky and whispers in his ear.

Lena and Darren both stop what they're doing momentarily, exchanging worried looks.

The chef moves from one cook to the next, whispering in their ears.

Bronko finally leans between the two of them. "They're all buying it, even the elders," he says gratefully. "They're all gobbling this shit up and acting like it's heroin. I can't even believe it."

He claps them both on the back hard enough to make Darren cough and Lena suppress a wince.

They send the entrées out excitedly.

Lena and Darren have actually managed to forget for whom and what they're cooking. It's become like every other catering gig they've ever been hired to chef.

And then there's an inhuman shriek of rage followed by a very human shriek of terror.

Then laughter.

Hideous laughter.

Lena looks up from the hotel pan full of paillards she's carrying between stations.

None of the other cooks (save Darren) so much as flinch.

Lena sets the pan down and runs to the archway, staring across the banquet hall.

There's blood on the wall, shining in one of Jett's designer light kits.

Its source is the newest busboy, or at least what's left of him on the floor.

By the time Darren joins a horrified Lena, Pacific and Mr. Mirabel are half carrying, half scooping what's left of

Raw Dog onto what looks to be a World War II–era military gurney.

They bear it out of the hall silently. Mr. Mirabel drags both the gurney and his oxygen tank on wheels behind him.

No one, including the two of them, seems the least bit disturbed.

Bronko is suddenly behind them, his arms around each of their shoulders, gently forcing them back behind the threshold.

"Easy now, kids," he coos to them.

Lena is breathless. "Chef, they just . . . they just . . ."

"It's a dangerous job," Bronko explains calmly. "Serving and cleaning up around demons, goblins. Things worse than demons and goblins. That's why I generally only hire the terminally ill or extreme sport adrenaline junkies who are gonna end up splattered on some rocks or in some field eventually when their chute fails anyway, like that poor stupid bastard they're wheeling out."

Lena looks at Mr. Mirabel, the old man with a head made bald by what she suddenly realizes is chemotherapy, perpetually tethered to his oxygen tank.

He suddenly makes perfect sense in this world.

Pacific does not.

Bronko sees her wheels turning as she looks at the kid and answers the question for her. "Pac is, uh, different," he says.

Lena looks up at him, her eyes more than they yet have grasping for some kind of mooring, be it moral or ethical or just plain rational.

Darren has reached the point where everything Bronko says becomes his mooring.

"Chef, how can you—"

"Tarr," he says firmly, "they all know exactly what they're getting into. They get hazard pay up the ass for it, and so do their families. How's it any different from signing up to be a soldier?"

Her eyes turn angry then, and that anger is only amplified by her inability to think of a counterargument at that moment.

"Look, the folks who don't expect to fall in the line of duty for their company are all back here, and we need to be grateful we brought them and us through this thing. Look out there. It worked. We saved ourselves, we saved Sin du Jour, and we saved something else. Something pure. Maybe the only pure thing you or I will ever touch. And you were a big part of that, you and your shy roommate over there."

His words are penetrating whether Lena wants them to or not.

She can't help feeling grateful.

She also can't deny feeling exhilarated by the whole

thing.

There's shame attached to that, and guilt, but Lena has learned to live with both of those emotions in abundance and continue thriving.

A horn whose bellow emanates from some long-ago era splits the air, drawing their attention, as well as that of the combined demon horde, to the main stage.

Joined by a herald wielding a massive trumpet made of bone, the Oexial general prepares to address the hall.

"Tell me now!" he begins with both arms raised. "Is peace between generations not worth a belly full of the rarest divinity known in the universe!"

Both Oexial and Vig'nerash cheer.

Rather than sounding joyful the sound makes Darren want to turn and run.

Because they're all demons.

"There is an Oexial tradition older than the light of this world," the general continues. "When Enochian fare is served at banquet, the last of us to taste of the flesh must judge its purity worthy of corruption in our bowels."

The Oexial soldiers all nod and growl their agreement.

The Vig'nerash warriors just laugh.

Dorsky's voice from the back of the staging area: "What the fuck did he just say?"

A split second later he joins Bronko, Lena, and Darren in the arch separating the hall from their antechamber.

“Everyone dummy up,” Bronko orders them immediately in an elevated whisper. “Not a word. Not a damn word.”

His eyes, however, are gutted and glued to the demon general on that stage.

“We have with us tonight a very special guest,” the general informs the hall. “He is the eldest of our clan, indeed the eldest to still draw breath among corporeal forms. He last sampled the forearm of Archangel Michael before the end of the first war. He will now sample the angel Ramiel, completing a circle within the Oexial clan that loops the whole of this world’s history and beyond.”

“Boss—” Dorsky warns.

Bronko just hisses sharply and unintelligibly at him.

“Brothers of the Oexial . . . new comrades of the Vig’nerash . . . I present to you . . . Astaroth! Third of the Fallen! Tempter of Saints! And High Elder of all Oexial!”

“We’re boned,” Dorsky insists.

Lena and Darren look to Bronko, waiting for his rebuke, waiting for him to disagree.

He doesn’t.

REFINED PALATE

He's the oldest living demon any of them have ever seen.

He's the oldest living *anything* Lena and Darren have ever seen.

Unlike the rest of the Oexial, who are draped in ancient cloth fashioned into mythic robes, Astaroth is even more old-school.

He's completely naked.

He's a hideous figure composed largely of wrinkles and filth. There are tufts on his mottled head that may be hair or may be cobwebs or may be something that exists beyond human explanation. All of his limbs defy symmetry, hanging at different angles and lengths from the sickly green sack of protruding bones.

It would all definitely repulse the chefs and staff, perhaps even permanently scar them, if they weren't suddenly preoccupied with the terror of their ruse being exposed.

Astaroth shambles into the hall through the main entrance, aided by two Oexial attendants.

The demons, both warrior caste and hierarchy, pound

the tables and make their horrible elated noises.

Allensworth and his people applaud politely, smiling.

Somehow they're more inhuman than the rest of the guest list.

Another Oexial attendant approaches Bronko.

"A fresh plate for the elder," he demands. "And choose a worthy cut."

"Of course," Bronko replies without hesitation.

He even smiles, flawlessly.

"Vargas, expedite that," he orders.

Darren doesn't move at first, not until Lena elbows him in the ribs. Then he's all nods as he retreats into the staging area, returning with a gleaming white plate.

Bronko takes it from him and hands it to the attendant, his smile never cracking.

Astaroth is led to the head of a table in the center of the banquet hall.

One of the attendants sets the plate with its perfectly grilled paillard before the elder.

"Dorsky," Bronko whispers to his sous-chef, "get a knife in everyone's hand. The big mothers. The Kramers. If the shit goes down, you and I are going to hold here. Tarr, you try to get everyone out the back. Run and gun. I expect you're the one to put in charge of that."

"Chef—"

"Just do what I tell you!"

Lena nods, her jaw tightening.

She knows how to follow those kinds of orders.

A moment later Dorsky is thrusting chef knives the size of small machetes with engraved blades into everyone's hand.

They wait.

Astaroth roughly shakes away his attendants, almost tipping over when left to stand on his own.

He addresses the hall, each word sounding like it's being spoken aloud for the first time.

"I have waited . . . an eon or more . . . to crush the light of such prey."

Another round of grotesque cheers.

He leans down with the weight and effort of eternity, and the movement seems to take that long.

He sniffs at the paillard.

His facial features are still recognizable enough for Bronko to detect a sneer, or what he perceives as a sneer.

The elder is handed a wickedly edged knife and a fork that appears to have been made for hay bales.

He stabs at the cooked meat, slicing through it with great effort.

Astaroth very nearly has to pry the bite past his shrunken jaw and onto his tongue.

He chews.

Every human in a white chef smock tenses.

Astaroth pauses midchew.

This time Bronko is certain the elder demon is sneering.

"A falsehood—" He swallows and shrieks in what can only be loosely categorized as a voice.

Then he stops.

Lena chokes up on the grip of her knife.

More than a few dozen sets of demon eyes turn their way.

She looks back at Bronko.

He shakes his head, watching the demon elder closely.

Astaroth's words seem stuck in his throat, along with the mouthful he just swallowed.

His black eyes are each as wide as a starless night.

He raises a knotted claw of a hand.

A single digit extends upward, as if he's about to make an important point.

At that moment Astaroth, first among Hell's hierarchy for longer than humans have recorded their history, keels over and all but breaks apart upon the stone floor.

It's clear even to those not familiar with the physiology of celestial creatures that he is suddenly one very dead demon.

He's still pointing.

No one is looking at the chefs now.

The silence is heavier and more menacing than a throng of Harpy shrieks.

Then: "Deceivers!"

"He is slain!"

"Poisoned!"

"Vig'nerash treachery!"

"Imp scum!"

"We didn't kill the old sack of offal!"

"No one wanted him here in the first place!"

"THEY HAVE MURDERED THE ELDER!"

"COME AT US, THEN!"

"BLOOD FOR BLOOD!"

The silence is replaced with bloodcurdling screams and guttural curses by the hellish choirful.

No one could possibly tell who strikes first.

It doesn't matter either.

In seconds tables are overturned, bodies are clashing upon bodies, and blood has streaked the floor and walls.

Oexial attacks Vig'nerash.

Vig'nerash attacks Oexial.

It's a full-scale demon riot.

"Back!" Bronko shouts at them. "Get back! Everyone!"

He spreads his arms and physically backs them all past the threshold of the staging area.

Fortunately, demons only seem interested in killing

demons.

"What the hell happened?" Dorsky yells over the commotion.

"I don't know," Bronko says, "but if he died because of our food, it won't matter whether or not they figure out what it was he just ate."

"Lena?" Darren says to her, barely keeping a grip on his blade.

She reaches out and grips his wrist, squeezing it reassuringly.

"What do we do, boss?" Dorsky asks.

Bronko seems at a loss.

A glass-on-glass clatter draws his attention behind them.

Pacific has dropped his large and encumbered rubber dish bin and is walking toward them.

He steps beside Bronko and serenely surveys the impromptu battle.

"Oh, right," he says, as if the information from his eyes and ears just hit his brain.

He looks up at Bronko.

"This is why you have busboys," he says, nodding.

PACIFIC BLUE

"No worry, brahs."

That's what Pacific says to them.

The demon melee has risen to a brimstone pitch and has filled every corner of the banquet hall. The youthful Vig'nerash soldiers are all banshee war cries and leaping erratic strikes met by the grizzled and growling determination of the Oexial veterans. Limbs and blood fly through the air in equal measure.

Worse, they've knocked over the buffet table.

A week's worth of Sin du Jour's blood, sweat, and tears is spread out across the stone floor, currently being mashed underfoot.

Pacific reaches inside his server's tunic and removes a plastic sandwich bag filled with pungent, vibrantly green herb.

"What're you doing, Pac?" Bronko asks the boy.

"Mo," he says to Mr. Mirabel with spacey grandeur, "the stash is yours now. Stay golden."

Mr. Mirabel accepts the baggie with slightly confused gratitude.

They all watch Pacific delve back inside his tunic and remove two pearly earbuds. Before he twists them into each ear, the sentimental circa-'70s English rock strains of Joy Division can be heard, muted, emanating from each.

With the same detached smile he always seems to wear, Pacific ambles off into the fray.

"Wait! He can't—" Lena begins to say, stepping forward to restrain the kid if necessary.

Bronko, who raises an arm in front of her as powerful as the iron bar of a roller-coaster car, stops her.

He says nothing, only shakes his head.

And despite the chaos and direness of the situation she could swear he's almost grinning.

Lena looks back at the battle, frantically searching for Pacific.

What she sees slows her racing pulse and baffles her brain.

It's as though he is somehow removed from time. The pace and carnage of the world around him never quite seem to touch Pacific. He Sunday-strolls through the melée without a care, without concern, and certainly without fear. He doesn't seem to follow any specific course, or ever react to the monstrous bodies thrusting into his path, and yet Pacific weaves deftly and perfectly between every obstacle and around any potential source of harm.

At one point he stops, bending over to pick up a goblet that has fallen and landed perfectly on its base, without spilling a drop.

At that same moment a stray demon's blade cuts the very same air Pacific's head occupied not half a second before.

Pacific stands, sipping from the goblet and then casting it aside as he walks on.

The goblet hits a Vig'nerash warrior who was moments from colliding with him in the face.

It causes the warrior to pause just long enough to be tackled by an Oexial soldier.

Pacific takes no notice.

He reaches the spot upon which Astaroth lays.

He kneels beside the ancient demon, casually.

Then he's obscured by a tableau of gnashing teeth, green flesh, and inhuman blood, all closing into the foreground.

Lena and Darren both look at Bronko, their expressions even more shocked than they were watching the demon elder keel over moments before.

"Two years he's been with us," Bronko explains. "Not a single scratch. It's some kind of natural gift."

"Homegrown," Mr. Mirabel adds, dipping his nose into his newly inherited plastic baggie and drawing a deep breath.

"We should bolt," Dorsky whispers hurriedly in Bronko's ear.

"And go where?" he snaps back with a frown.

"All hold!" the booming, magically enhanced voice of what must surely be the Devil himself commands.

And all do, however briefly.

The leaders from each demon faction have taken to the stage together.

The Oexial general is holding a talisman to his lips, through which he speaks.

"All hold, I say!"

The clashing slows to a few particularly enraged combatants, who are then broken up by their fellows.

The banquet hall quiets.

The same all-encompassing voice: "Make way!"

The sea of sudden combatants parts as the leaders descend the stage and move in a processional across the banquet hall.

They form a semicircle around Astaroth's shriveled body.

From where the chefs are standing, none of them see Pacific.

The Oexial robes and the Vig'nerash suits confer over their eldest elder, leaning close to examine his form.

Allensworth and his people stand in the background,

observing without comment.

However, even Lena and Darren can recognize the veiled concern on Allensworth's face.

After long minutes marked by Bronko and his people's sweat and the ticking of their nervous feet, the conference between demons ends.

When they return to the stage, the Oexial general speaks without his talisman.

"The cause is natural!" he announces. "There was no poison, no foul play. The elder's time has come! Our Lord of Winged Fire has called him home! Cease your bloodlust and let us celebrate his passing to the eternal side of the Fallen!"

A chorus of horrifying cheers breaks out from Oexial and Vig'nerash alike.

Bronko finally exhales in relief.

The rest of the chefs take their cues from him, standing at ease for the first time in what feels like days.

"So all that means we're good, right?" Pacific asks.

The chefs spin around.

He's standing beside them, preparing to spark a joint as thin and miniscule as a toothpick perched on his lower lip.

Bronko reaches out and snatches the blunt before it touches fire.

"What the hell, Pac?"

Pacific looks up at him as if noticing him and the joint for the first time.

"Oh. My bad, boss."

"What happened out there?"

Pacific reaches into his pocket, peering around carefully as he does, and slips something discreetly into Bronko's palm.

"The old monster dude choked on that," he explains. "I pried it out of his mouth and palmed it before anyone got to him."

Bronko places the object against his chest, covered, and deftly lifts one edge of his hand to peer inside.

"No fucking way."

"What is it, Chef?" Dorsky asks.

Bronko slowly and carefully lowers his hand, turning his back to the banquet hall.

They gather around him.

Each set of eyes peers into his hand and the object it cradles.

It's a chicken bone.

It's a chicken bone that's been gnawed on repeatedly by very small canine teeth.

It's a chicken bone precisely like the one Sin du Jour's recent stray Shih Tzu mascot has had in its mouth for the past three days.

In fact, it is that very same bone.

"Is that—"

"Yes."

"The fucking dog's bone?"

"How did that get into the food—" Darren begins to ask.

"Not Boosha," Bronko says, and it's meant for his ears and thought process alone. "She would never. The dog, though . . ."

Lena can't even begin to accept that. "Dog?"

Bronko's slow deduction is abruptly replaced by intense alarm.

"We have to get back to Sin du Jour," he says. "Now. We have to go."

Pacific waves them off easily. "You guys head back. We'll clean up."

But Bronko is already gone.

Lena and Darren look at each other, then they hurry to catch up with him.

Dorsky watches them all depart.

He sighs.

"Shoulda just cooked the fucking thing," he grumbles, walking slowly after them, in no particular hurry.

When the chefs have all retreated from the edge of the banquet hall, Mr. Mirabel wheels his oxygen tank alongside Pacific.

"I ain't giving you back your stash, you know."

Pacific shrugs. He reaches inside his tunic and produces an identical plastic baggie.

"I just wanted to leave you something, brah."

Mr. Mirabel laughs until he's hacking into the palm of his hand.

"Easy, Mo," Pacific bids him, patting the older man lightly on the back.

"You little prick," he manages through another, lesser series of coughing.

Pacific grins. "I love you too, pal."

DOG

Bronko very nearly takes the front doors off their hinges as he storms Sin du Jour's lobby.

By the time Lena and Darren have caught up to him, the chef is already running through the halls.

Passing the main kitchen, a single blinking image stops him in his tracks.

Bronko peers inside, simultaneously awestruck and repulsed.

Ritter, Cindy, Hara, and Moon are all gathered around one of the many freestanding stations arranged in a perfect grid.

Its stainless-steel surface is covered with paper bags bearing the Henley's logo.

Having heard the story in detail after the team rested and cleaned up, Bronko can't believe what he's seeing.

Moon is currently jamming his face into a Henley's Double Udder almost bigger than his head, red pepper–flecked skirt steak hanging from the toasted sourdough bun like a grotesque tongue.

Ritter is dipping clown noses in ketchup while Hara

plucks one Nuggie after another and pops them into his mouth with disturbing rhythm.

Slightly removed from them, Cindy eats a green salad from a plastic carton.

"Seriously?" Bronko says to them, his breathing ragged.

Ritter shrugs. "We had a craving."

"Most of us," Cindy corrects him.

"Yeah, and they might not be making this shit much longer," Moon adds, sauce staining his lips and cheeks like blood.

Bronko opens his mouth to comment further, then simply shakes his head and begins running down the hall.

Lena and Darren trot after him.

At that moment the rest of the kitchen staff has arrived and is discovering the front doors rattling in their frame.

A few minutes and a dozen winding hallways later, Bronko reaches the apothecary with Sin du Jour's newest chefs on his heels.

It's empty.

Boosha isn't there.

More importantly, the angel isn't there.

Most importantly, the angel's serving cart prison *is* still there.

Bronko walks over to the trolley upon which Ramiel

was bound with a spell more powerful than anyone employed by Sin du Jour could either conjure or break.

All that's left on its surface is a nondescript dog collar with a tiny, equally nondescript tag attached to it.

Bronko picks up the collar, squeezing it tightly in his hand. "Son of a bitch."

"Did they take it?" Darren asks. "Did they find out? Did they know?"

"I don't know, kid," Bronko all but whispers, hopelessly. "I don't know."

A gentle melody suddenly draws all their attention.

They look to the door as Boosha shuffles into the room, humming quietly to herself, appearing undisturbed.

"Where the hell were you?" Bronko demands.

"Looking for Dog," she says, either not picking up on his tone or not caring. "Must have gone back to streets. Is sad. He was sweet dog."

She stops, peering behind them at the empty trolley.

"Angel is gone," she observes neutrally.

"No shit, Boosh."

"Language!" she hisses.

"Fuck that!" he snaps at her, throwing the collar down onto the trolley. "My people went through hell to save that thing! Where did it go? Who took it? And what about that dog, or whatever it was? It used us to whack a demon elder! Who sent it?"

"It did kind of save our asses, Chef," Lena points out.

"Whatever! I don't like being played, and I don't like being used!"

Lena squints past Bronko at the surface of the trolley. She steps past him, reaching down and picking up the dog collar.

She pinches the tag between two fingertips and reads it closely.

"Holy shit."

Bronko turns to regard her. "What? What is it?"

Lena actually ignores him. "Boosha? Are you, uh, dyslexic by any chance?"

"What means 'dyslexic'?"

"When you read words, do you sometimes get them backwards? Mixed up?"

Boosha folds her arms and tilts her chin back. "Only human words," she says defensively.

Lena slowly nods.

"What the hell are you talking about?" Bronko asks, more insistent this time.

Lena looks up at him.

Darren is marveling at her expression.

He's never seen her truly dumbstruck before.

"This tag," she says. "The Shih Tzu's tag. It doesn't say 'dog.' Boosha reversed the 'D' and the 'G' when she read it."

Lena hands the collar to a confused Bronko.

He takes it, examining the tag for himself.

His entire face seems to sag at once.

"Oh, come on!"

"I don't get it," Darren says. "What?"

Lena looks over at him.

She waits silently.

It hits him twenty seconds later.

His expression mirrors hers. "Oh my god . . ."

Bronko sighs, closing his fist around the collar and sticking it against his hip.

"Yeah," he says. "Apparently so."

Acknowledgments

I'd like to thank Lee Harris, my editor, who makes the post-writing process fun and who I believe is as close to a Whedonverse Brit as one finds in the real world. This book and series also owe a debt to Alasdair Stuart and Marguerite Kenner, both of whom saw it along at a very fragile time. My mother, Barbara, who remains my most fervent fan and most vocal cheerleader. My brother-from-another-mother, Earl, always a source of encouragement. My webmaster, Helljack, for his years of tireless online support. I'd also like to acknowledge all the folks who supported my first novella series, Slingers. They kept my head in this form and my hopes for it alive. Finally, although the book is rightfully dedicated to her, I must acknowledge the contributions of my lady, Nikki, with whom I plotted all the menus in these stories and who offered much more beyond just the food. I couldn't have done it without her. I couldn't do anything without her.

About the Author

Photo credit: Earl Newton

MATT WALLACE is the author of *The Next Fix, The Failed Cities,* and his other novella series Slingers. He's also penned more than one hundred short stories, a few of which have won awards and been nominated for others, in addition to writing for film and television. In his youth he traveled the world as a professional wrestler and unarmed combat and self-defense instructor before retiring to write full-time.

He now resides in Los Angeles with the love of his life and inspiration for Sin du Jour's resident pastry chef.

TOR·COM

Science fiction. Fantasy.

The universe.

And related subjects.

*

More than just a publisher's website, Tor.com is a venue for **original fiction, comics,** and **discussion** of the entire field of SF and fantasy, in all media and from all sources. Visit our site today—and join the conversation yourself.

Made in the USA
Middletown, DE
30 March 2020